HER HOCKEY SUPERSTAR FAKE FIANCÉ

A Strong Family Romance Companion Novel

CAMI CHECKETTS

Birch River
PUBLISHING

COPYRIGHT

Her Hockey Superstar Fake Fiance:

A Strong Family Romance Companion Novel

Copyright © 2019 by Cami Checketts

FREE BOOK

Sign up for Cami's VIP newsletter and receive a free ebook copy of *The Resilient One: A Billionaire Bride Pact Romance* here.

You can also receive a free copy of *Rescued by Love: Park City Firefighter Romance* by clicking here and signing up for Cami's newsletter.

PROLOGUE

Faith Summers dodged around slower-moving fans, who were simply trying to leave the hockey arena after an exhilarating win by the Vail Mountaineers, 4–1. Faith had a much higher purpose than exiting the rink where Vail High played their games. She had to get to the glass so her boyfriend, Jag Parros, would see her as he did a victory lap. She always waited on the other side of the plexiglass with her gloves pressed against it, ready for their tradition.

At the bottom of the bleachers, she squirmed past a few people and slammed herself against the glass. There he was. Jag had his helmet off, and he and his teammates were making their way around the outside of the ice, waving to fans as they went. As center and captain of the team, Jag was loved and respected by his teammates and high school fans alike.

He drew closer, and her stomach did that funny roll every time she saw him. Her smile grew as she pressed her gloved hands to the glass, waiting impatiently for him to spot her. His dark hair curled slightly from the sweat, and his handsome face was approaching. It wasn't just his incredible looks that drew her in. Jag was crazy fun and made her feel like the most important person in the world.

He spotted her and his face broke into a huge grin. "Faith," she could see him mouth. He skated right next to the plexiglass, slamming into it and making her jump.

She laughed and cussed him. "Jag!"

He put his gloves right where hers were on the glass. It was their sign that nothing could come between them, neither the glass nor the distance he would have to travel to make his hockey dreams come true. She could see his lips form the words, "Love you."

"Love you back," she said.

They were only seventeen years old, and her parents had expressed concern that she was not only too young to know what love really was, but that Jag was going to leave the valley soon and never look back. They were wrong about the former and right about the latter. Well, hopefully he'd look back for her, but she knew he was destined for greatness.

"Wait right there," Jag mouthed carefully, his body pressed against the glass as his teammates had skated on without him. Some fellow high school students were watching their exchange, but she didn't care.

"Right here?" she asked back.

He nodded and mouthed, "Don't move."

Faith returned the nod, acting very serious. She kept her gloves on the glass as he skated backwards, watching her with a mischievous grin. Finally, he turned and zipped to the team's exit and locker room. Faith let out a breathy sigh. How she loved him.

"You two are ridiculous. You know that, right?" Blaine Grainger, Jag's closest friend, was standing next to her, giving her a wide grin. Blaine was a well-liked, good-looking guy who always seemed to be one step ahead of the rest of the crowd, and that had helped him become the student body president. Faith didn't have an issue with him, but quite often felt like he was too brilliant for her to keep up with. She aspired to be a hairdresser, while Blaine aspired to be a lawyer and a judge. Different paths. She only hoped she and Jag weren't on different paths as well.

"Yep. Ridiculously in love," Faith shot back.

"I hope deeply in love." He smiled, but something in his voice unsettled her. She had no clue why. Blaine was a great friend to Jag, but a few times he'd gently reminded Faith that Jag would be moving on without her. An unsettling look in his eyes made her wonder if he looked forward to that day.

"What do you mean?" She took her gloves off the wall and turned to face him. The stadium was emptying now, and she and Blaine were almost alone.

"Faith …" His smile disappeared. He looked out at the empty arena and muttered, "I'm sure Jag will tell you tonight. I told him he needs to."

Her stomach pitched and she pressed a gloved hand to her abdomen. "Did he get in?" She'd been hoping and praying for Jag to achieve his dream of attending the Patriot Academy, an exclusive hockey prep school in Massachusetts. They all knew he was too good of an athlete for their small high school in Vail, Colorado. Jag and Faith actually lived twenty minutes away in the picturesque valley of Lonepeak, but they came to the larger high school in Vail so Jag could play hockey and she could be on the swim team.

Blaine nodded shortly. His gaze swung to her, as if wondering if she'd collapse.

Faith's legs did feel weak, and her head swirled with the warring emotions of happiness and despair. She wanted Jag to have his dream of playing in the NHL, wanted it so badly for him, but as she'd feared, she was being left behind. Jag's parents could afford to relocate to Massachusetts to be close to him. Faith's parents were dairy farmers and couldn't even afford her swimming fees. She worked all summer to pay her fees and to buy a few school clothes so she didn't look as poor as they were.

She didn't know how much time passed as she tried to process it all. Jag would leave her next fall. She'd miss him, but someday, somehow, they'd be together. She knew it. Jag knew it.

The compassionate look on Blaine's face said he definitely didn't know it. Blaine wrapped a comforting arm around her, and she leaned against him. It felt like one of her rowdy brothers calming down enough to hug her and support her. "Sorry, Faith. I know how it feels."

"Being left behind?" she murmured.

"Yeah."

He didn't say any more, but she knew the story. His mom had ditched his dad when Blaine was only five. His dad had worked hard to become a successful businessman and was now the mayor of Vail. He'd remarried recently and seemed happy. Blaine appeared successful and well-adjusted also, but Faith had seen something in his eyes, something that made her hurt for him. He often went with Faith and Jag on double dates, always bringing a different girl. She hoped he found someone who was right for him some day.

"I'm sorry," she muttered.

Blaine pulled her into a full-on hug, rubbing his hands up and down the back of her thick sweatshirt.

"Hey!" a loud voice roared from behind them.

"Jag!" Faith yelled happily, tearing herself from Blaine's embrace, turning and running pell-mell at her favorite person in the world.

Jag's face was full of concern, probably from seeing his girlfriend in his best friend's arms, but it quickly changed to his normal wide grin as she flung herself at him. He caught her easily and swung her off the ground. Faith wrapped her arms tight around his neck, holding on and planning to never let go. Not until he left her in the fall.

Her smile slipped and she clung to him, burying her head in his neck. She smelled his warm, musky cologne. How would she survive without him? Senior year was bound to be lonely, as would the years following, until he established himself, they could get married, and she would move wherever he had committed to play hockey. The thought of leaving her little valley, her parents, and her younger siblings hurt, but nothing hurt as much as the thought of being apart from him. A rogue tear slid out and escaped down her cheek.

Jag set her on her feet and leaned down to kiss her, but stopped short. "What's this?" He gently lifted the tear off her cheek, then looked to Blaine for an explanation. "What did you do?" he demanded.

Blaine held up his hands and backed away. "It was time, dude. Man up and tell her the truth."

Jag's brow furrowed. His blue eyes turned stormy. "I was planning on it, but not like this."

Blaine rolled his eyes and turned to go, throwing a parting shot over his shoulder. "Don't worry, Jag. I'll watch out for her." He turned and strode out of the arena.

Jag held her more tightly, as if the thought of anyone but him watching out for her cut deep. "I'm sorry," he breathed against her cheek. "I was planning to tell you tonight."

Faith tugged off her gloves, dropped them, and wrapped her palms around his smooth jawline. "Jag, don't be sorry. I'm thrilled for you."

"You are?" His voice sounded uncertain and husky.

"Of course I am. This is your dream. Go get it."

"You're amazing, Faith. Of course you'd be happy for me."

"Why shouldn't I be? I'm the proudest, most obnoxious girlfriend you've ever seen."

He grinned. "I wish I could watch you in the stands while I play."

She ran her hands up into his hair, loving its soft wave. Truthfully, she loved everything about him. "You'd be embarrassed for me. I scream like an out-of-control Jag junkie."

"I love it." He let out a low groan. "If I could just take you with me, everything would be perfect."

She laughed, though her gut churned when she thought about leaving the valley and the people she loved. "I think both our parents would object to that."

"Mine wouldn't," he insisted. "They adore you."

"What's not to adore?" She winked sassily.

Jag chuckled and bent down close. He tenderly kissed her, making the now-deserted stadium seem to light up with fireworks. She savored each kiss they shared, and they'd shared plenty.

Jag put their hands together and said, "Nothing will ever come between us. Nothing."

Faith believed him. She smiled and nodded, willing the tears to stay away. She was happy for Jag, and she wouldn't hold him back, no matter how it hurt.

Jag released her hands, lifted her off her feet again, whirled her around, and pressed her up against the glass.

She grinned. "I might have to give you a penalty for boarding, Parros."

He chuckled. "It'd be worth it."

He claimed her mouth with his, pushing all worries over him leaving far away. Long, wonderful minutes later, the janitor had to pull them apart and ask them to leave, not for the first time. The janitor grinned and teased with them as he did so.

Jag took her hand and led her from the stadium and to the bonfire party waiting for them up the canyon. They loved each other. No matter how many miles and years separated them, that wouldn't change. Just like their gloves on the glass, nothing could separate them. She wouldn't let it.

CHAPTER ONE

Ten and a Half Years Later

Faith rushed out the door of the spa at Angel Falls Retreat, only briefly stumbling as the brisk winter air threatened to knock her backward. She zipped her coat and upped her pace. She'd had a walk-in haircut come in at the last minute, and now she'd be late for practice; she was the coach of a competitive youth swim team in Vail, but it was twenty minutes away and practice started in eighteen minutes. Pulling her phone out, she started typing quicker than she walked, asking the assistant coach to start warming the team up without her.

"Oof!" She slammed into something hard and large. Bouncing back, she hit the pavement on her rear, pain radiating up her backside and her phone skittering away underneath a parked car. Glancing up, way up, she saw a man towering over her. The sun was bright reflecting off the snow, so she couldn't quite make out his face, but his body was tall, lean, and beautifully muscled under a fitted long-sleeved shirt.

"Faith?" he asked.

Her stomach did a funny flip-flop it hadn't done in years. When that voice said her name, she found herself diving back into dreams she'd long since stored and tried to forget. Those dreams were nothing like reality, as she'd buried her husband Blaine a year ago. Her life for over ten years now was far removed from Jag's deep, husky, beautiful voice saying her name.

The man bent down low and swept her off the ground. Thankfully, her thick coat dampened the impact, but excitement and heat still shot through her as she was lifted face to chest with the man who dominated her night dreams, no matter how many times she'd prayed to stop dreaming about him. If she had any money, she'd hire a therapist or voodoo witch doctor to exorcise him from her memory.

"Faith," he repeated, saying the name this time almost reverently. Jag's handsome face looked all lit up. He appeared for all the world like the boy she used to adore, grown into an irresistible man with hard lines and firm muscles and yet a softness in his eyes as he gazed at her.

He lifted her off her feet, without her permission—and much to her body's happiness—and swung her around like he used to do. Setting her back down, he was still grinning at her. "Faith." How many times could he say her name in different ways? This time it was a husky groan. She knew exactly what was coming when he said her name in that way, and she wanted him to capture her lips more than she wanted her swim team to win state this year.

He bent down close, his blue eyes taking her in as if she were his entire world. His muscular body surrounded her, and for the first time in years, she felt safe. Any moment now their lips would connect, washing away all the pain and misery she'd been through these past ten years disappear, and Jag would make everything right in her world.

"And who is this?" a snarky voice asked from his side.

Jag wrapped Faith tight and turned her, as if to shelter her from the woman standing next to them. Faith peeked over his muscular arm to see a gorgeous redhead in a tight business suit that pushed her well-endowed front out for the world to enjoy. Faith worried that the woman would get frostbite on her beautiful front alignment. It was chilly out here.

"What are you doing here?" Jag demanded.

The woman smiled silkily. "You know exactly why I'm here: to finish the story I was promised an exclusive on."

"You weren't promised it by me. Butt out of my life, Sheryl."

"Oh, but I can't. You're my ticket, Jag, and we both know you owe me much more than a story."

"I don't owe you anything." Jag looked back down at Faith. The tightness in his brow and mouth eased, and he said, "Sorry about the interruption. Give me a second, and we'll continue."

Faith had been so enthralled by his presence, followed by the intriguing conversation between him and this picture-perfect woman, but now all the memories and the pain came rushing back and she squirmed to be out of his embrace. With a rush of horror, she realized she'd almost let him kiss her. They weren't going to simply pick up where they left off. Never. Jag had ditched her ten years ago. She had moved on—well, as much as a woman desperately in love could move on. She now loathed him almost as much as she'd adored him.

"I'm late for swim practice," she grunted out, thinking of something that he would respect so he would let her go. She didn't have the time or the energy to tell him off properly for leaving her and never so much as writing her a letter.

Well, that wasn't true. He'd written her the one letter asking her to let him go so he could be successful, but she hated that letter too much to think on it. His prep school had been very strict and not allowed any electronics. He'd been able to write hand-written letters, though, and by the time he'd been there one week, she'd sent him a dozen. When the long-awaited letter from him arrived a week after he'd officially left her, she'd ripped it open and his words had ripped her heart in two. She'd sent him a final letter and never heard from him again, even on breaks when he could've tried to at least call and remedy the rift between them.

"I'll follow you there," Jag told her, as if he had any right to follow her anywhere.

Faith shook her head in frustration, dropped to the ground to fish her phone out from under the car, and then practically ran to her beat-up Corolla.

"I'll be there soon!" Jag called after her.

She ignored him, unlocked her car with trembling fingers, and dropped into the seat. Typing out a shaky text to the assistant coach to start without her, she managed to start the engine and putter away. As she glanced back in her rearview, she could see Jag watching her go, even as the redhead chattered away at him a mile a minute. Faith tried to focus on the road, but the look of longing on his handsome face about had her running into a service truck.

Clutching the steering wheel tightly, she forced her gaze away and forced her concentration to the road leading away from the resort and past town. She had to head out of the valley and to Vail for practice, and she was late. Yet her mind couldn't even comprehend that worry. She was too focused on the man she'd just seen, the man who had held her as if no time and heartache had passed. Jag Parros. He'd come home after ten long, lonely years. Why? The more important question was: How would her heart survive?

J ag ignored Sheryl Boden's flapping jaw as he watched Faith leave. Her long dark hair streamed behind her as she ran to her car, slipped inside, and then drove away. He'd held heaven in his arms for a few short seconds, and then she'd ditched him again. He'd thought he was over her. He'd paid a lot of good money for therapists to root her from his mind. But apparently one encounter could make him revert to his seventeen-year-old self, desperately in love and idealistically thinking they'd end up together again, no matter how long or hard the road was to get there. He was stupid around Faith Summers. Irrational and stupid.

He could still feel her lean form in his arms, see her dark eyes staring up at him and those perfectly full lips all soft and ready to meet his. Dang Sheryl for interrupting. She was doing her level best to ruin his career, but that was less upsetting than this interrupted kiss. Almost ten years without Faith's lips meeting his, and Sheryl had ruined it. Big surprise—Sheryl ruined everything she touched.

He forced himself to look at her. He'd made the mistake of dating her last year, taken in by the smart, beautiful redhead. As always, he'd tried to find a woman who could push Faith's memory out of his brain, but it never worked. Now he knew dating Sheryl was the biggest mistake of his life, next to not leaving school and coming after Faith after she'd coldly written him off the first month and never responded to any of his letters after that.

"What do you really want, Sheryl?" he asked, folding his arms across his chest. It was chilly in Lonepeak Valley, but he was used to that, living on the ice. People strode past them. The Angel Falls Retreat and the attached ski resort was run by his friend Nick's family, the Strongs. It was busy this holiday weekend. When his mom had asked if he could get away for Christmas for a few days, he'd suggested they come here. There had definitely been an underlying hope that he'd see Faith, but he hadn't dreamed it would be this incredible and powerful.

"You." Sheryl gave him what was probably an alluring smile to some, but it made him sick to his stomach. "And the story, as always."

"You're trying to set me up," he said in a low voice. He wanted to discreetly get his phone out and record her answer, but he doubted she'd reveal the truth.

She laughed, and he wondered how she wasn't freezing in that tight-fitting, thigh-high suit with her chest spilling out. "We both know there's more to the story, that you would never have thrown that game." She tapped him playfully on the chest, and he stepped back out of her reach. Her smile dimmed, but she didn't give up. Sheryl Boden didn't know the meaning of the words *give up*. "I just want to get to the bottom of the story, clear your name, make you look good ..." Her voice lowered and she stepped in closer again. "And resurrect the love we once had."

Jag was thinking quickly. He needed a way out of this.

When he'd taken this five-day break for Christmas to get away from Boston, his agent had agreed and told him, if possible, to find a way to get some good publicity. He'd almost collapsed at the game a few days ago. They'd determined that his weakness was due to the flu, but after several tests, the doctors had revealed a worse diagnosis: he had multiple sclerosis. It had blindsided and terrified him. The only good news was that the disease could take years to manifest. He could keep playing if he could keep himself strong and keep the coaches, the team owner, and the press from knowing the truth, especially the snarky woman in front of him. What she would do with the info, he didn't want to imagine. Either she'd gain more interest for her career, or she'd blackmail him. He'd bet on the latter.

There was a lot of speculation that he'd thrown the game against the Islanders when his strength had given out and he'd had to finally pull himself from the game. What a crock. A self-respecting Bruins player would never let the Islanders win. More worryingly, his five-year contract was up for renewal this year. Five years was the average length of an NHL career, but he knew he had a lot more years in him. He hated hiding his disease from his coaches, but he couldn't give them any reason to not re-sign him. Hockey was his life, especially since Faith had ditched him.

Sheryl was watching him expectantly.

"You're going to have a boring Christmas," he muttered. "You've got nothing on me."

"The speculation on you throwing that game is through the roof. Did someone bribe you?"

Jag rolled his eyes. He had plenty of money and would never succumb to a bribe.

"I know you're here for your parents' anniversary and Christmas. Reunion with the whole family back in the valley you were raised in. So sweet."

Jag had to hand it to her: she had her sources and she was good at digging out the truth, or her version of the truth. He wanted to get away from her and chase after Faith. How was it possible that Faith was even more beautiful than he'd remembered? Anger shot through him as he thought of the years of missing her, wondering why she'd turned from him, and then finding out that she'd fallen in love with his old friend, Blaine. The two had married a couple of years ago, after Blaine finished his law degree and returned to Vail, settling in Lonepeak Valley to be close to Faith. Blaine had died last year, a year before tomorrow, actually. Jag still felt guilt that he hadn't come to the funeral, but he'd had a game that day and he honestly didn't know if he could stand seeing her or staring at Blaine in a coffin. He didn't hate the guy, just felt insanely jealous that Blaine had what Jag had always wanted: Faith.

"Who's the woman?" Sheryl asked, a bite to her voice.

Jag smiled, and an almost giddy feeling washed over him as he thought of Faith. "My fiancée," he said. As soon as the unplanned words slipped out, he felt even happier—there was a rush of heat at the mere suggestion of being married to Faith, and he longed that the words could be true. When he'd seen her again and held her, it had been like no time had passed. They'd been kids, seventeen years old, when it had all fallen apart. He wanted to pry the story out of her, why she wrote him off, why she married Blaine, and what she'd been up to the past ten years. Some part of him felt like they still had the same connection, like she'd just been here waiting for him.

Sheryl's mouth went wide, and then fire traced through her green eyes as her mouth tightened. "That's a lie," she hissed.

"No, it's not," he insisted, his gut scrambling. They'd been basically engaged at one point, but now it *was* a lie. Sheryl could ferret out a story wherever she went, but maybe this little unplanned slip could get Sheryl off his back, make her realize they'd never get back together, and she'd bug somebody else this holiday season. He had to get to Faith now and beg her to pretend to be his fiancée, until he could hopefully talk her into it for real.

He beamed at the idea of Faith being his fiancée, and this would make his agent happy, too. An engagement to a beautiful sweetheart like Faith would definitely look good. Stable, religious, kind, fun, beautiful … he could list good qualities about Faith all day long. An engagement story could also distract from the rumors of him throwing that game or being washed up.

"If you'll excuse me, I want to go see my fiancée. You should go find a juicier story this Christmas." He waved sarcastically at her, then turned and ran for his rented Audi. He wouldn't put it past Sheryl to follow him, but he had a head start and he knew where he was going. He had to somehow talk Faith into the fake fiancée idea before Sheryl caught up to him.

His parents weren't expecting him for dinner until seven. With any more luck, he'd be bringing Faith back for dinner with them. His mom and sister would be ecstatic.

CHAPTER TWO

Faith stewed how she was going to deal with Jag being back in town. Even though she drove ten miles over the speed limit, she made it to practice fifteen minutes late. She apologized, and some of the older students, the preteens, razzed her about swimming extra laps like she'd make them do. She shook off the worry and excitement of Jag and promised them that tomorrow she'd get in the water with them and swim those extra laps. She loved being in the water and joined them often, but most of the time it was easier to coach from the pool deck.

Half an hour into practice, a man strode through the exterior door and into the waiting area. He was a tall, well-built man with dark hair that curled slightly at the ends, bright blue eyes, and her heart in his hand. Dang him all to heck.

She couldn't peel her eyes away from the glass separating them from the reception area. He spoke with the receptionist briefly, and then he was striding through the door and catching her eye.

His own eyes lit up, and he grinned. She noticed a scar next to his lip that hadn't been there in high school. She'd been too distracted and surprised to notice earlier today. She wanted to find out how he got that scar, right after she kissed it. No! She had to be strong.

Forcing her eyes away, she watched Jasmine slide through the water doing the breaststroke. She could shave some seconds off her time by getting a little more strength to her kick. Faith would recommend some weight-lifting moves Jasmine could do on their non-water practice day.

Faith studiously avoided looking at Jag, but she could sense him approaching, as if they'd never been apart and she was still as attuned to him as ever. Then he was standing by her side, attracting stares from some of the kids who were taking breaks or were out of the water. She heard Tyler, one of the older boys, breathe, "That's Jag Parros. Holy crap!"

"The hockey player?"

"Yeah, man."

"Tyler." Faith's voice was more of a bark than she'd ever heard it. "Get moving."

"Yeah, Coach." Tyler cast one more look at Jag, then dove under and started across the pool, doing freestyle.

Faith didn't look at Jag. She didn't know if she was strong enough to look at him and not throw herself into his arms again. Without a coat on like earlier to block some of the sensation, she'd be in major trouble. He eased in closer to her, and his musky smell mingled with the strong chlorine scent from the pool. She'd been raised in the water and was addicted to Jag's scent, so she found herself leaning toward him also.

He leaned so close his mouth tickled her ear and sent darts of desire through her. "That's Faith Summers. Holy crap," he murmured.

Faith laughed. She couldn't help it. She loved him teasing her and loved that he still called her by her maiden name. When Jag's deep chuckle joined hers, she let herself look at him. He grinned down at her, that easygoing grin that she'd thought was the highest reward any woman could ever hope for in life. He was tough on the ice, but he'd always been funny and soft for her.

"You look amazing, Faith," he said, brushing some hair away from her face and making her jaw tingle from his soft touch.

"You look amazing-er," she admitted.

His grin just kept getting bigger. He lowered his voice and said, "We need to talk."

All the tingly good feelings disappeared. She focused back on her team and called out some commands and instructions. The last thing she wanted to do was "talk" with him. He was the one who'd written her that letter dismissing her and their relationship. The letter hadn't been harsh, just truthful: he was going places and couldn't tug her along. It had still ripped her apart. She'd loved him with all her seventeen-year-old heart. She'd never recovered.

Eight years later, she'd finally let Blaine talk her into getting married. He'd been very kind to her and very patient, but she'd never fallen in love with him like she'd hoped she would. Then, a year later, Blaine had died of a brain tumor. One day he was healthy, and the next day he had intense headaches and was rushed into the emergency room and diagnosed. Three weeks later, he was gone. Tomorrow was the one-year anniversary of his death. He'd written a letter the day he was diagnosed with the brain tumor and asked her to read it at the cemetery on his one-year death day. It had been sitting on her dresser, taunting her, for a year. She was curious but a little leery of what it would say. Did he know she'd never loved him like she did Jag?

Anguish and guilt rushed through her. She'd married Blaine knowing she still loved Jag. She'd wasted her life and her marriage, unable to get over the man standing next to her. Now he had the gall to show up after leaving her for almost ten years and want to talk? No way.

"I've got nothing to say to you," she muttered. "Go, go, go!" She raised her voice to yell at Nancy. "Great job!" she called as Nancy finished the sprint lap.

"Well, I've got enough to say for the both of us."

She glanced up at him. It was a mistake. He was so stinking appealing. She wanted to either throw her arms around his neck and kiss him, or shove him into the pool.

"I need your help." His voice was urgent. "There's this reporter that's after me."

"The lady in the tight suit?" she asked, arching an eyebrow. So he'd only come after Faith for some help? That stung. Was that lady the kind of women he dated? "Enjoy it." She forced a fake smile.

"No. Honestly. There's nothing enjoyable about this. I need to stay far away from her, and I need to look good for the media." He lowered his voice and said, "So I lied and told her you and I were engaged."

"You what?" Faith yelped.

The pool fell silent, except for the splashing of those swimming who didn't hear their coach's outburst.

"Sorry," Faith said somewhat calmly to her team. "Sorry. You're all looking great. Keep … swimming." She turned back to Jag. "Why would you say that?" she hissed through her teeth.

He smiled easily. "Because I've always wished it was true."

"Excuse me?" Her heart was thumping out of control. Emotions warred within her: anger that he would dare say something like that, and an out-of-place desire since she also had always wished it could be true. She'd wanted him for so long, and now he had the guts to show up and try to use her to look good for the media. Before he had a chance to say more that would either anger her or make her want him, she shook her head. "No way. I'm not pretending to be engaged to you."

"Please, Faith. I need your help, and you owe me."

"I owe you?" Her voice was pitching up again. "How dare you?"

He splayed his hands, looking for all the world as if she had misused him. "I'd think after breaking my heart ten years ago, you'd want to make it up to me."

"*I* broke *your* heart?" Each word was louder than the last. Faith couldn't stop herself: she shoved him into the water.

Jag yelped in surprise, flailing his arms and trying to grasp for something, but he only reached for air. He hit the water with a loud splash.

The members of her team were either staring at her in shock, laughing, or talking rapidly to each other. Nobody was swimming. Jag surfaced, his expression vacillating between shock and amusement. He looked even more incredible with his dark hair dripping water into his face and his clothes now plastered to his muscular body.

"Practice is over!" Faith yelled. "See you after the break." She turned and speed-walked toward the entry. They had a two-week moratorium starting tomorrow. Maybe it would be long enough for the kids to forget how their coach was acting right now. She doubted it.

"Faith!" Jag hollered.

Faith ignored him and broke into a run, grabbing her purse and coat from the bench and ignoring all the chattering of her team behind her.

She figured she'd made her point with Jag. No reason to stand around and discuss it further. She scrambled through the icy parking lot and into her car, started the engine, and peeled out of there. As she glanced at the rearview, she saw Jag sprinting out of the front doors. His clothes were dripping, and she could see he was yelling for her to stop. Faith laughed at the famous, ultra-handsome man standing there soaking wet. Her laughter faded quickly. Maybe she'd won this round, but Jag wasn't one to quit easily. The only thing he'd ever quit was their relationship.

Tears pricked at her eyelids. She brushed them angrily away and stepped on the gas. She was just upset because it was the anniversary of Blaine's death tomorrow. Jag's presence had nothing to do with it. The lies she told herself didn't help at all. Jag was the most excitement she'd had since he'd left, and knowing he was only going to leave her again was far worse pain than losing her husband. That was a horrible thing to even think. She wished she could push it away, but truth wasn't easily dismissed when you were lonely and hadn't felt true love for almost a decade.

J ag watched Faith's crappy car speed away, screaming her name, but she didn't stop. He wanted to run after her, but he'd already made enough of a spectacle of himself. He wrung water from the bottom of his shirt, pushed a hand through his wet hair, and then pulled his cell phone out of his pocket. This phone was supposed to be waterproof. He hoped so.

He stomped to his car, half ticked and half amused. She'd pushed him in the water, which he could laugh about, but how could she feel justified in acting all ticked that he'd said she hurt him? She'd about broken him in two with her rejection letter, asking him to not contact her again. He'd written her a dozen letters that were never answered. At seventeen he'd been prideful and hurt, and that pride had festered. He'd also been in a private school where they didn't allow cell phones, so he hadn't had much choice to go after her, but now he was a full-grown adult in charge of his own life, and he knew what he wanted—that beautiful lady who'd just shoved him in the pool and run away.

As he got close to the Audi, it beeped and unlocked. At least the key still worked. Opening the door, he ripped off his shirt and tossed it in the passenger's side. He settled into the driver's seat, held on to his phone, and tried to think who he could call to help him find Faith and talk some sense into her. He had lost contact with most of his friends from the valley, especially after Blaine betrayed him and pursued Faith. Jag hated to think that they'd been married. The thought of Blaine touching her made his stomach sour.

Nick Strong. Nick was the one friend Jag had kept in semi-contact with, mostly because Nick had also gone away. The year after Jag left, Nick had gone to college and enrolled in the military. He might not respond, but Jag did have his email, and earlier today he'd seen Faith coming out of the spa at the Strongs' resort. Maybe Nick could give him the number of whichever brother ran the resort. Gavin. That was it. At least it was somewhere to start.

Jag drove back toward Lonepeak Valley and the Angel Falls Retreat where he, his parents, his sister, and his brother-in-law were all staying in nearby suites for the Christmas holidays. Jag only had four days before he had to be back for practice on the twenty-sixth and a game on the twenty-seventh. Four days to enjoy Christmas with his family. More importantly, four days to get to the bottom of Faith's anger and twisted view of how she'd hurt him.

His multiple sclerosis diagnosis had been weighing heavily on his mind, but right now he needed to get Faith to talk with him and —if someone in heaven loved him—kiss him.

J ag realized his problem as soon as he carried his wet shirt and walked through the front doors of the lodge at Angel Falls. Sheryl hadn't followed him, but she was obviously waiting for him. Luckily, she was tapping away on her phone and hadn't looked up when he entered the building. He couldn't make it to the elevators past the restaurant on the main level without being spotted, so he opted for the grand staircase to the second level.

As he crept toward the stairs that were only ten feet past the front desk, he caught the receptionist staring at him. Her eyes were wide, and she was obviously ogling his chest. Jag raised a finger to his lips. She blinked at him but then slowly nodded, grinning. Jag returned her smile, hoping she wouldn't say anything and draw Sheryl's attention this way.

He reached the staircase and was on the fourth stair when he heard Sheryl shriek, "Jag! What happened to your shirt?"

Jag whirled and lifted a hand. "Just went for a swim with my fiancée. She's a swim instructor. That's why she's so perfectly shaped." He grinned as her mouth pursed and her eyes narrowed.

He turned and pumped up the stairs. Making it to the second level, he darted for the bank of elevators across the way, but he didn't dare wait. There was an exit sign and he barged through that door, relieved to find stairs. He ran up the next five flights. He was in the best shape of his life—the multiple sclerosis hadn't affected him yet, and the doctors believed it would be slow progressing—but he was out of breath when he burst out the door and into the sixth-floor hallway. He darted to his room, wanting nothing more than a shower and a way to find Faith again before dinner.

The door next to his swung open and his younger sister, Brielle, walked out. She was a beautiful brunette with dark eyes like their mom. He'd gotten his blue eyes from his dad.

She stopped short and lifted her eyebrows. "The chest is built, my brother, but do you need to display it everywhere you go?"

Jag rolled his eyes, pulled out his soaked leather wallet, and retrieved his key card. "I get better publicity that way," he told her.

"Now that I believe. What happened? You're dripping on this beautiful hardwood floor."

Her husband, Mason, a tall redhead, appeared behind her. They were both dressed nicely for dinner. "Hey ... what happened, dude?"

Jag's door beeped and he pushed it open. Should he admit the truth? Brielle was a few years younger than him and had always idolized Faith. She asked him so many times why they'd broken up that he'd finally forbidden her from saying Faith's name.

Jag drew in a breath, focused on Brielle's pretty face, and said, "I saw Faith."

"You did?" Brielle hurried to his side and put her hand on his arm. "Was it sparks again? Is she still beautiful? Does she still love you?"

Okay, he'd made a mistake telling her. Brielle would hound him until Faith was in his arms again. Yet that was the end he wanted too, so maybe the pressure from his sister wouldn't be too bad. "The first two questions, yes. The last ... doubtful."

"Ah, bro. Too much time has passed. You tragically messed up your own life by never chasing her down. Sometimes I seriously despise you."

Jag looked to Mason. "Come on, man, help me out. Bro code requires you stop her when she gets like this."

Mason chuckled. "You've known her longer than I have. Maybe you have the magic button to stop her."

"I'll stop you both," Brielle warned with all the sass a little sister should have. She was annoying but fun to tease, and he'd missed her since she'd gone to school in Kentucky, met Mason, and gone off to live in Atlanta. "Now spill it all."

Jag shook his head. "I ran into her coming out of the spa, but she left for swim practice. I lied to this horrible reporter that I was engaged to Faith, and then I chased after her to try to collaborate with her on the story. I found her at swim practice in Vail. She got ticked when I said she'd hurt me, and then she pushed me in the pool."

"Wow." Brielle's eyes were wide. "That's a story. Why did you lie about being engaged?"

"It just came out, but I have to get this stupid reporter off my back." He hadn't even had the chance to tell his family about his diagnosis. He would eventually; he just hated the thought of growing weak and having anyone know about it. Burying it for the time being made it less scary somehow.

"And Faith was mad that you said she'd hurt you?"

"Yeah. Go figure, right?" His family had relocated to Massachusetts when he'd gotten accepted into the Liberty Academy. Brielle was one of the few he'd confided in about Faith ripping his heart out.

"Something is messed up here, bro."

"Yeah. Me still being in love with her and now dripping all over this hardwood floor." He pushed out a breath of disgust. "I'd better go shower so I'm not late for dinner."

Brielle nodded. "Okay, okay. Mason and I will make a plan for how you're going to win her back, because if she got that ticked, then obviously she was hurt and thinks you're at fault. Right?"

"Isn't the man always at fault?" Mason piped up.

"Aw ..." Brielle kissed him. "You finally got it right. I love you."

Jag shook his head. They'd been married in June and still acted like annoying newlyweds. "Going to shower now."

They were still kissing. Mason waved him away.

Jag hurried into his room, dropping his wet clothes on the bathroom floor. As he finally got under the warm spray, he couldn't push something from his mind. Faith had acted like she'd been hurt and he was at fault, but how was that possible? She was the one who'd written him off and then never responded to him. He had no answers as he dressed for dinner and hurried to be with his family, but at least he was here and had a chance to sort things out. Then again, if Faith was mad enough to yell at him, and then shove him in a pool, maybe he didn't have a chance.

CHAPTER THREE

Faith got into work early the next morning because she was planning to leave at four and go to the cemetery. She probably should've planned some kind of death day wake, but she just wanted to be alone and read the letter. For some reason, she'd dreaded the letter.

The day Blaine had been diagnosed, he hadn't said much. They'd finally arrived home, and he'd gone right to the office and wrote the letter. He'd placed it on the bedroom dresser and asked her to please wait and read it on the year anniversary of his death. What he possibly wanted her to know that needed to wait a year was beyond her. It was almost like he wanted her to have that time to distance herself from his death and be prepared for whatever he wanted to tell her. So many times she'd almost read it, but Blaine had always been devoted to and in love with her and she'd never felt the same. The guilt that came from that made her want to at least honor his last wish.

The spa was busy, as usual. Many women were coming in wanting their hair to look good for Christmas. Others were treating themselves before the holidays with massages or pedicures. She was the only hairstylist on staff, as many people came into the spa looking for pampering-type treatments rather than a haircut. She still stayed plenty busy. Most of her clientele was vacation-based, as only a few regular customers could afford the more expensive spa. Also, a lot of families came to stay at the Angel Falls Retreat year after year, so she'd sometimes get return customers. She specialized in cut and color, but she also did nails and sometimes filled in for pedicures where needed.

The spa was beautiful with views of the mountain and valley. All glass walls in the main area were one-way, so they could see out but the passersby couldn't see in. The treatment rooms were enclosed and private. Faith had her own area, but it was more of a cubby than a completely private room. She liked that, because she could hear the water feature from that spot; the water feature made up the wall of the spa that separated the main part from the treatment rooms. She'd always loved water and swimming, and that constant sound of a waterfall, echoing the Angel Falls that the retreat was named after, soothed and uplifted her.

This month, Christmas decorations had taken over the spa and the entire Angel Falls Retreat. It made everything even more beautiful and picturesque. Sadly, her sudden status as a widow last Christmas had ruined the holidays for her. She simply wanted to get through it. With Jag here this year, Christmas felt different, exciting, and new.

She was putting in the last few foils for highlights on a sweet lady from town who rarely stopped chattering. Faith didn't mind, as it let her mind wander to all things Jag. Last night, he'd been the superstar of her dreams. This morning, she'd kept an eye out for him. Was he staying at the lodge with his family? She thought he'd said that. She'd always adored his mom, dad, and sister. She'd heard Brielle had gotten married, and she would love to see all of them, but she didn't know how to deal with Jag being around. Why exactly had he lied to that reporter that they were engaged? Fire raced through her at the thought of being engaged and married to Jag. Did beautiful dreams like that really come true for some people? Not for her.

"Faith? Faith?" Nessa from the front desk had her head poked around the barrier and was calling to her.

"Oh, hey." Faith patted down the foils covering Mary's head and peeled off her gloves, tossing them. "We're going to need that color to set for at least half an hour," she told Mary. "Let's get you under the dryer." She led Mary over to the seat with a warm air dryer and got her started before turning to Nessa. "Sorry. What did you need?"

"Can you squeeze in a man's haircut?"

"Sure. That'll be about perfect timing for Mary's color to take."

"Perfect." Nessa looked back over her shoulder and gestured with an inviting grin.

Faith pasted on a smile to greet the client. When a tall, dark-haired man walked around the barrier, her stomach flip-flopped and her heart threatened to pound out of her chest. "You?"

Jag grinned, looking innocent, attractive, and mischievous all at the same time. "Hi, Faith."

"You good?" Nessa asked, her brow raised in query.

Faith started to say no, but Jag said quickly, "Yes, thank you," strode to her chair, and sat down. He glanced up at her, still grinning like the cat who'd caught the canary. "Just a trim, please."

Faith gritted her teeth and pulled out a clean drape. How was she going to get through the next half hour washing his hair and then massaging his scalp, brushing close to him as she cut his hair? With any other client, it wouldn't bother her at all, but the sparks she felt every time she was near Jag were impossible to ignore.

She fanned the drape and let it fall around him. Securing it around his neck, her fingers brushed his skin and her face heated up as he sucked in a breath and stared up at her. *Oh my goodness!* How was she going to get through this without heart failure or plopping herself on his lap and begging him to love her again?

She glanced away quickly under the guise of checking on Mary. Sadly, Mary had a *Rising Star* magazine in hand and was oblivious to anyone else in the world.

"How are you doing?" Jag's voice brought her around.

"Fine," she said briskly. "You?"

Jag's smile wasn't quite as brilliant now. "I meant today. How are you doing with today? The anniversary ..."

Faith felt the remembrance like a punch in the gut. "None of your business," she grunted out.

"I'm sorry about Blaine. He was a good man."

She acknowledged this with a nod, but she could tell it was hard for him to say. She and Blaine had never mentioned Jag's name in their home, as if even mentioning him would tear them apart. It probably would have. "Thank you. Can you please just let me do my job?"

Jag's smile was gone. He nodded.

Faith spun his chair around and lowered it so his neck rested on the pad on the sink. She got the water warm and took a few steadying breaths. He was just a haircut. She'd done hundreds, possibly thousands of haircuts, and she'd never had untoward thoughts. She could do this.

Her fingers started working the water through his hair, and the sensation of touching him was as warm as the water on her skin. Her hand trembled slightly. Jag could never be just a haircut, and she was in deep, deep trouble.

J ag hated that Faith didn't want to even give him a chance to talk. He'd hated Blaine for stealing her, even though she hadn't been Jag's for a long time, but then he'd felt immense guilt when he'd heard about his old friend's tumor and sudden death. He'd never wish losing a beloved husband on anyone, especially not on someone that he cared so deeply for. But it bugged him that Faith hadn't really even accepted his condolences.

She lowered his chair back, and he was staring up into her gorgeous face. He loved her slightly upturned nose, her smooth skin, and the dimple in her right cheek when she smiled big. She hadn't smiled big since he'd seen her again. What if she never smiled big anymore? That was a gut punch, and he wanted to change it for her.

Her long, silky hair brushed across his neck. He could smell that hint of vanilla, and it all rushed back: how desperately he'd loved her, how much fun they'd had together, and how she'd always been meant to be his.

The warm water hit his head at the same time that her fingers started running through his hair. Jag held in the moan of pleasure, but only just barely. After a few seconds, she turned the water off, filled her palm with shampoo, and started working that into his hair. She massaged his scalp and even his neck so thoroughly that he was tingling all over. He loved every second of her hands on his head, and he may or may not have let out a soft groan. Maybe she couldn't express it in words and maybe she was mad at him for some unfathomable reason, but she still cared for him. It all came through her fingertips and her standing so close and being so sweet with him.

He couldn't imagine she felt this way about anyone else, but then a horrible thought hit him. His barber in Boston had never given him an intimate massage as he shampooed his hair, but what if this was standard process for Faith? What if she did something sweet and amazing like this massage for every client?

His eyes flew open. She was staring down at him, but she averted her gaze.

"Do you do this with every client?" he demanded.

"Excuse me?" Her dark eyes came back to his face.

"Do you give every client this sexy and amazing massage? Is that part of a haircut for you, or are you just doing it for me?"

Faith's eyes widened, and she pulled her hands back and started the water again. She rinsed his hair thoroughly and didn't answer him. Quickly working some conditioner into his hair, much less thoroughly than she'd done with the shampoo, she rinsed his hair again and then wrapped it up in a towel. She put his seat back up and said snippily, "Just a trim, then, sir?"

Jag nodded shortly, annoyed and frustrated. Why had she sweetly and beautifully massaged his hair—getting so close, smelling so good, making him forget the past ten years of being apart—and then got all offended at his simple question?

She dropped the towel in a bucket and started combing and snipping away at his hair, going out of her way to avoid touching him. That ticked him off even more.

"Can you please answer my earlier question?" He had to stare at her in the mirror, because she was behind him now.

"Which was?" She arched an eyebrow, all impertinent and adorable.

"Is the massage standard procedure for a haircut?"

"Yes, sir, it is." She glared at him. "But most people understand that and don't make a big deal out of it."

His own eyes narrowed. He stood quickly and spun to face her. Strands of hair dropped onto the floor from his robe thingy, and her eyes widened in surprise. "So you're telling me that you sit and massage each man who comes in here? All sexy and alluring?"

Faith clung to her scissors, glaring up at him. The lady sitting underneath the upside-down bowl didn't even look up from her magazine. "Would you stop it?" Faith asked. "Many hairdressers give a scalp massage as part of the haircut. It doesn't mean anything, and nobody but you has ever reacted like this."

Jealousy turned his gut as he thought about her hands all over other men, especially Blaine, but maybe she was right. Maybe no one else freaked out like he was doing because no one cared as deeply for her as he did, and no one else was meant to be with her like he was. "Maybe I reacted like that because your touch does something special for me," he blurted out.

Faith's eyes softened then. She studied him for a few beats. Her tongue darted out and moistened her full lips, making his heart-beat roar in his ears. He wanted to move around the chair, tug her close, and finally have her lips under his again. He'd missed her for many long years. Luckily, hockey had kept him insanely busy, because right now he didn't know how he'd survived without being close to her.

"Maybe," she finally admitted.

Jag felt himself soften. He smiled and pushed away the jealousy and the ache of missing her. "Thank you for the massage," he murmured.

"If you sit there quietly and let me cut your hair, I'll give you another massage after I'm done."

"Really?"

"Can you sit there quietly?"

Jag grimaced. He wanted that massage. He wanted her fingers on his scalp, but he wanted to talk things out even more. So many years, and maybe there were misunderstandings that once resolved could clear up some of the pain. Nothing could take away the pain and betrayal of her writing him off and then later marrying Blaine, but if he could be with her, he could overlook that. "Okay," he finally conceded.

"Okay." She gave him a partial smile—not the full-dimple smile, but enough encouragement for him to sink back into the chair.

She kept combing, measuring, and snipping, but he could feel that something had changed. Instead of leaning away from him, she was leaning in. Her arm would press softly into his back or shoulder or chest, and he'd get that heady scent of vanilla. He loved it. He kept his promise not to talk, but that didn't mean he couldn't stare at her. And stare he did. He drank her in as she focused on his hair. He'd catch her eye and give her what he'd been told was his smoldering glance. She'd blush and look away again. He loved those interactions almost as much as her brushing against him and smelling irresistible.

She put down her scissors and ruffled his hair as if getting the stray strands out. Then she filled her palm with something that smelled good and started working it into his hair. He wanted to keep his eyes open and stare at her, but this scalp massage felt so unreal that he had to close his eyes and just let himself savor the sensation.

After not nearly long enough, her touch went feather light, and she pulled away and used the comb to brush his hair to the side and away from his face.

"Please don't stop," he murmured, "That was amazing."

She smiled, and he got a quick glimpse of that dimple. "Sorry. I've got to rinse Mary's hair out, or she's going to look like a skunk." She tilted her head to the lady under the inverted bowl, who was still buried deep in her magazine.

"Can I see you later?" he asked quickly before she pulled away completely. Standing, he turned to face her.

"I ... I don't know, Jag."

"Please, after work. Let me take you to dinner, take you out for ice cream, take you ice skating, take you to Iceland, anywhere ... please."

She gave him a little half smile and her dark eyes seemed to be interested in him, but then she pushed the words out quickly: "I'm going to Blaine's grave after work."

"Oh." He grimaced and looked away. He and Blaine had been close once, but he couldn't imagine how hard it would be to go to the grave and watch Faith mourn for the man she'd chosen to marry instead of Jag. Not that he'd even been in the running when she'd married Blaine, but it still felt like the two of them had betrayed him. At the same time, the thought of her suffering hurt him. If only he had the right to hold her and comfort her.

"Do I pay you or up front?" he asked, instead of begging her to let him come, let him be there for her no matter how much it hurt. Because that was what you did when you loved someone as much as he'd always loved Faith. The tension should've crushed them, but when he was spending time around her, it all came rushing back even stronger, as she was all woman now and he couldn't hide the longing he felt for her.

"Up front."

He nodded. "Thanks. The massage was amazing."

She smiled then, but it wasn't a soft smile that meant he was going to get a kiss. It was the smile of her needing to leave but hating to go. At least it meant she still cared. "I'm glad you liked it."

Jag felt like his time with her was slipping away, like the awful moment in the spring when the ice started melting on the lake and there was nothing you could do to stop it, or when a puck somehow got past his stick and was racing toward the opponent and all he wanted was to get it back. He didn't even know where she lived or what her phone number was. He could stop by her parents' place—they'd always been kind to him—but would they want to give out information about her? "Do you still live with your parents?" he blurted out.

"No." She rolled her eyes. "What kind of a loser do you think I am?"

Jag laughed, despite how churned up he was inside. "I didn't mean it like that." He took a deep breath and admitted, "I wanted to be able to find you later."

She studied him, then walked away, lifting the bowl thing off Mary's head and escorting her to the seat Jag had vacated. Faith didn't give him much. Her lips were pursed like they used to do when she was thinking deeply. Jag stood by, feeling like she didn't want to push him away but she had no choice. Was her memory and longing for Blaine too strong to let Jag back in? Whatever it was, Jag hated it more than he'd hated losing to the Islanders.

Mary smiled at him, tinfoil sticking out all over head.

"Hi," Jag said.

"Hiya, handsome." She gave him a wink.

Faith laughed and gave Jag a conspiratorial look. The intimacy of shared humor washed over him, filling in the cracks that had opened when she'd dumped him ten years ago and soothing them—to a point. Nothing could really fill them or heal him until she agreed to be his again. Did he even have a chance?

Faith put some gloves on and started pulling the foil things off of Mary's head. Jag figured he was supposed to take this as his cue to leave. He could come back tomorrow and get his own head covered with tinfoil, but he didn't want to wait until tomorrow.

"Please," he said in a low tone.

"I ..." Faith's brow wrinkled, and she stared deeply at him. Her dark brown eyes were beautiful and appealing.

Jag begged her with his own gaze. He felt her leaning his way. Was she was going to cave? He prayed she would, but nothing in her gaze told him which way she'd go. He used to be able to read her every mood. He wanted to put his hands up and see if she'd match them with hers, no matter if there was no glass and no gloves.

She shook her head, focused back on Mary, and said in a murmur, "Today's just not good."

His hopes crumpled, but he knew she was right. He knew he needed to back away. "Tomorrow?" he asked quietly.

She shrugged and met his gaze, her dark gaze infusing some hope into him. "Maybe."

The last of Mary's foils were pulled out, and her hair looked crazy: a sickish yellow in spots, red in others, and even black here and there. It looked as unstable and messed up as he felt right now. Jag didn't know what else to say or do. Maybe he was wrong, absolutely wrong, and he and Faith weren't meant to be together.

Or maybe it was like fighting his guts out to get into UMass and then get the notices and offers from the pro scouts. He hadn't given up then. Why would he give up on something so much more important than hockey? He'd given up on him and Faith years ago, but he'd been immature and stupid back then. He'd been lost without her, but he'd deluded himself into thinking that he'd be okay, that he'd someday find someone else. Now he knew better. Now he knew there was no one out there like Faith. Not for him.

Faith leaned Mary back in the chair and started rinsing her hair. Jag watched carefully, and he knew that this hair rinsing was nowhere close to the way Faith had massaged and rinsed his hair. All the crazy colors started washing down the drain, and he saw that Mary's hair was going to be okay, pretty even, with different twists of highlights. Maybe he and Faith could be okay.

Faith glanced up at him. "See ya, Jag," she said softly.

Jag lifted a hand and backed away. Today wasn't good. He got that. Maybe tomorrow. The way she'd washed his hair had been special. They had a chance to blend together like Mary's hair. He was waxing weirdly philosophical, which was completely unlike him. He waved to Mary and then strode around the little barrier and to the front desk to pay. Faith worked at a nice place. Tomorrow he could see her, maybe do something with her, maybe talk. That should be good, but he only had a limited amount of days before he'd be back in Boston, across the country from her again.

He hated to wait, especially because he had nothing to do. His entire family was up skiing, and he couldn't ski, as per his contract. What was he going to do with himself for the rest of the day? Nick had helped him get Gavin's number earlier, and Gavin had helped him get in contact with the spa and figure out exactly when Faith would have a sort of break to fit him in. It had worked pretty well. Maybe he'd bug Gavin again and see if he could go ice skating on the lake behind the Strong's house. The long day stretching out in front of him needed to be filled, or he'd go crazy waiting to see Faith again.

CHAPTER FOUR

Faith had struggled through work, counting down the hours and then the minutes. It was so unlike her. She loved people and loved helping them feel more appealing. She was a natural with hair and had always loved doing it up for her little sisters and their friends. For the rest of the day, all she'd wanted was to go find Jag again. She couldn't let herself do that. Today was supposed to be about Blaine, honoring and remembering him on the anniversary of his death. She would finally get to read that letter, and maybe that would help her move past all the hurt and loneliness.

The letter was in her purse, and she was planning to go straight to the cemetery in Vail after work. She thought it was very sad and telling that she'd rather go knock on doors in the lodge until she found Jag rather than face whatever Blaine wanted to tell her. Blaine had been persistent in his pursuit of her, until she'd finally married him because he'd always been there for her and constantly promised that he loved her enough for the both of them. He'd always been very, very kind to her. He'd treated her like a china doll. She'd hated it, and she'd felt extremely guilty that she'd hated it.

Rushing out the door, she hurried through the near-full parking lot toward her car. Angel Falls Retreat was busy this Christmas season, and now that it was December twenty-third and school was out, there were large groups of local families and teenagers enjoying the slopes, as well as the crowd of out-of-towners who were staying at the resort for the holiday.

She waited for an Audi sport utility to pass by. It stopped right next to her instead. The window rolled down, and Jag was smiling at her. "Fancy meeting you here."

Shaking her head, she couldn't hide her own smile. "Have you been driving around the parking lot just waiting for me to walk out?"

"How low you think of me." Jag grinned. "Honestly, I haven't. I hiked up to the Strongs' lake, and I've been ice skating all afternoon."

"You and that lake."

"It's my happy spot. Can you ... wait right there?"

"Right here?" she asked.

"Don't move."

Faith laughed, and all the angst over the letter and Blaine's death day disappeared as she remembered how often Jag had said those exact words after one of his hockey games while she waited at the glass. How she wished she could've gone to his college games, and how she wished she could now go cheer at his Bruins games.

Jag pulled into a stall, jumped out, and hurried over to her. "Can I walk you to your car?"

"I guess so." She smiled up at him. He was so tall, so handsome, so perfectly perfect.

He put a hand on her lower back and escorted her to her car. The sun was shining bright today, and with her coat on and Jag by her side, she felt as warm as summertime.

They stopped next to her beat-up Corolla. Blaine had bought her a nice Jetta after they'd been married, but the twenty percent of his medical bills that weren't covered by insurance had motivated her to sell everything she could. She was proud that she had no debt and could make the payments on their house; she didn't need a nice car.

Faith set her purse in the car and turned to face him. Jag shut the door and leaned in close, so that Faith's back was pressed against the car. He placed both his hands on the roof of the car, effectively pinning her in. Her breath shortened. They'd been in this position before, and she knew exactly what was coming next.

She stared up at his face. Jag's blue eyes were focused deeply on her. He shifted closer, and his strong body pressed against her. Faith forgot about everything but him. She should slow down. She should exercise some self-control. Instead, she lifted her hands and framed his face with them. It was cold outside, but that didn't matter. She was safe in the warmth of Jag's arms again, and nothing and no one could hurt her.

She trailed her thumb along the scar next to his mouth. "How'd you get this?" she murmured.

"Fight on the ice." He smiled. "My helmet came off and the ice ripped my lip open."

Faith slid her arms around his neck, stood onto tiptoes, and softly touched her lips to the scar.

Fire raced through her as Jag turned toward her so their lips were aligned and murmured, "You missed."

Faith smiled, lifted her eyebrows, and said, "You gonna help me with my aim?"

"Yes, ma'am."

Anticipation and a heady desire swirled around them as Jag's lips hovered over hers. She wanted him to kiss her, take command of her world, and push away the ten years without him.

Jag smiled slightly and moved in.

"Can I get a statement from your fiancée about how you met?" a snide voice asked from much too close by.

It was the redhead reporter lady. She was dressed a little smarter today in a formfitting ski coat and pants. Faith had been curious about her yesterday. Today she was ticking her off.

Jag cursed softly and ushered Faith's head to his chest, holding her close as if to shelter her from the woman. "There will be no statement, and if you keep this up, I'll sue you for harassment."

The woman laughed. "I'd love to see you waste your money."

"Go bug some idiot who wants the publicity," Jag said.

She only laughed louder. "You want it …" Her voice got husky. "All of it."

Faith couldn't believe what the woman was implying. She pulled from Jag's grasp to glare at the woman.

The redhead smiled and said, "I know all about you, Faith Grainger. Betrayed Jag and married his best friend. Blaine died a year ago today. So tragic. So *desperate*, aren't you, sweetheart?"

Faith's temper flared at the woman's condescending tone. That woman had butted into their almost kiss and conversation, and she was being a complete brat. Faith wanted to tell her off, but she could sense that claiming Jag as hers would bug this woman more than anything. Faith gave her as cold of a smile as she was getting. "Back off from my fiancé, or I'll show you Western hospitality like you've never seen."

The woman arched her delicate eyebrows, her green eyes cunning. "You're way out of your league, sweetheart." She tsked her tongue and looked at Jag. "A widowed hairdresser driving a rusted-out Toyota. Classy. Your fans are going to love this. Is this an engagement for charity or simply a long-lost love?"

Jag started toward her. The menacing look on his face would've scared his teammate, Josh Porter, who loved to fight more than he loved to score.

The woman scuttled away. "I think I've got plenty to whet the people's appetite. See you soon."

Jag watched her go, turning back to Faith with a heavy breath. "I'm sorry," he muttered. "Sheryl has it in for me."

"I got that." The moment between them was shattered, leaving her upset and unsteady. This was Blaine's death day, and she'd all but thrown herself at Jag. What was wrong with her? Being around Jag scrambled her brain waves, leading her to make rash, crazy decisions. They weren't engaged; they didn't have a future. She needed to remember that, and quick. "I've got to go," she murmured.

Jag nodded, studying her as if he wanted to convince her to stay but knew he shouldn't. "Can we talk later?"

Faith shrugged and backed away. Pulling the car door open, she used it as a barrier between them. If Jag touched her, she'd come unraveled and could easily forget her own name. "There's too much between us," she said.

"I know." He grinned. "Sparks and happiness and me never wanting to let you go."

Faith trembled from his words and the warm look in his eyes. She felt the exact same way, but ... "That's not what I meant. Too much garbage and pain, Jag."

Jag didn't come around the door, but he leaned over it, getting much too close for her susceptible heart. "We can work through it, Faith. We have to be able to."

Faith didn't know about "have to." "And then what? You leave me again, write me off with a lame letter?"

"Excuse me?" His eyebrows dipped together. "*I* wrote *you* off?"

Faith clung to the door, anguish and anger rolling together at the memory. "You broke my heart, Jag. I know I was young and probably too immature, but I loved you, and you dumped me for hockey."

"I didn't dump you; you dumped me," he protested.

Faith glared at him. "Get your story straight, Parros. Maybe your reporter friend can help you." With that, she dodged into her car, slammed the door, and started it.

Jag stood there, glaring down at her through the window. She thought maybe he'd try to stop her, but it looked like he was as mad as she was. How dare he claim she'd dumped him? Maybe ten years had dulled his memory or he'd taken one too many hits to the head. Jerk anyway. As she pulled out, she couldn't resist looking in the rearview mirror. The anguish on his face cut deep and made her abdomen clench. She forced herself to look away and push on the gas. Jag couldn't even admit that he'd dumped her and apologize. A simple apology would go a long, long way. He lived in a high-dollar, delusional world—a world she'd never been a part of and never would.

Tears streaked down her cheeks as she drove to the cemetery. She wished she could claim they were tears for her deceased husband.

"A little fight with the little woman?" Sheryl asked.

Jag whirled on her. "Stay away from me," he muttered, pushing past her and hurrying toward the lodge.

"Is that the statement you want me to print when your career already seems a little shaky?" Sheryl called. "Or do you want me to tell everyone that your fiancée is a gold digger who hugs you one minute and screams at you the next? She seems a little unstable."

Jag stormed back to her. If a man had said that, he could and would knock the guy on his butt. With Sheryl, he had to be smart and use other weapons. "You dare share anything unsavory about her, and I will hire a private investigator to dig up dirt on you and make sure your name is laughed at in literary circles."

Sheryl shrank back from him. It would probably be easy to find mud on such a slimy creature. He couldn't believe he'd ever thought she was attractive.

Turning, he stalked away from her. Sheryl had ruined another near kiss with Faith. Worse, Faith had gotten all upset with him again. He'd admit that he shouldn't have let her go years ago; he should've pursued her harder. But how could she claim he'd written her off when it was the other way around?

He hurried into the lodge. He needed to shower and find his family. Tomorrow was Christmas Eve, and he wanted to be with them. If only he could have Faith with him as well.

CHAPTER FIVE

Faith was shaking by the time she reached the cemetery twenty minutes away in Vail. She couldn't lie to herself and say she didn't love Jag anymore. She loved him so much that she wanted to spin her car around and go track him down, kiss him, and beg him to talk through the past ten years of pain and separation. The only thing keeping her from doing exactly that was the letter in her purse. She had to read it. She had to give Blaine at least that much. He'd been good to her, and she hated that she'd married him because of how much he loved her, how persistent he'd been, and how lonely and miserable she'd been with no hope of Jag ever coming back into her life.

Parking on the strip of asphalt a hundred yards from Blaine's grave, she pulled the letter out but left her purse, phone, and keys in the car. No one would bother her here. She sank almost up to her knees in the snow as she made her way to the grave. Her stylish ankle boots were no match for the cold, especially when snow fell down in them. She burrowed her face deeper into her coat and kept moving.

After she read the letter, she'd go have a proper cry at home in front of the fireplace with some cocoa. Tomorrow was Christmas Eve, and being around her large, loud family was exactly what she needed. She suspected that after reading the letter tonight, she'd just want to be alone.

Finally, she reached the grave. Her eyes traced over the engraving on the large gray marble headstone: *Blaine Richard Grainger. May 20, 1993 – December 23, 2019. Beloved husband, brother, and son.*

That was it. It was simple. Faith had wanted to put some person-alized details on it, but his dad was a very stern man and he preferred it clean and "classy." Faith didn't fight him, knowing that his dad, stepmom, and half-sisters grieved him much more than she did. At moments like this, the guilt of not loving her husband like he'd loved her almost overwhelmed her.

She was freezing, so she figured she might as well get on with it. She broke the seal on the envelope and slid the letter out. Her fingers were trembling, partly from the cold, mostly from the worry about what the letter might contain.

She pulled it out and realized something before she even started reading. She'd never read a handwritten anything from Blaine. He always had joked that everything was online, and why would you write when you could type? She'd seen his signature but never his script. It looked oddly familiar, though, probably because she knew him so well.

Dear Faith,

If you're reading this, it means I've been gone for a year. The news of my brain tumor scared me today, petrified really. To know that I had a matter of days or weeks to be with you and then I'd have to leave you behind ... I love you so desperately that the thought of being without you feels like somebody has already ripped my heart out.

Faith looked out over the frozen cemetery. She hated that she'd never felt that depth for Blaine, not even close. She'd thought of him as a best friend and had tried for years to convince him that he deserved someone who loved him as much as he loved her, but he always affirmed that he wasn't worthy of her and loved her enough for both of them. Her heart ached at his loss—not just because he'd died, but also because she often felt like he'd wasted his life being so devoted to her when she never fully returned the feeling.

I'm not afraid to go to heaven. I feel ready to meet my maker, and my conscience is clear. Except for one thing.

Her interest perked up. The ever-perfect Blaine had something he'd done wrong? He was always smart, deliberate, and straight as an arrow. She'd never even heard him say a curse word.

Do you remember when Jag left for the Patriot Academy? Of course you remember. You loved Jag almost as much as I love you.

Wow. Once Jag left town, Blaine had wanted to deny that Jag ever existed. Now she was more than intrigued; she was excited and scared to read what he had to tell her. His conscience was pricked because of something he'd done to his old friend?

You know I've loved you since I was twelve, so what I'm about to tell you might not come as a surprise. The night at the rink that you found out Jag was leaving and you let me hug you ... That day I knew we were meant to be together and I'd do anything to make you mine. I pray you'll forgive me for what I did.

Faith's stomach tumbled, and her trembling fingers paradoxically felt stiff.

When I found out Jag couldn't have any electronics at prep school, couldn't text or call you except for at Christmas, spring break, and summer break, I saw my opportunity. I did something ... underhanded. I intercepted the letters.

Now her heart was racing faster than her eyes were devouring the letter.

I had a friend who worked at the post office sorting mail. I paid him to take all of Jag's letters before you got them and intercept yours before they went out. Then I wrote the letter from Jag, the one where he dumped you, sealed it back in his own envelope, and snuck it into your mailbox. Then, if you'll remember, you confided in me that he'd dumped you and you were such a mess. I waited for you to write him off, and then I told you I'd get the letter to the post office. I took it and altered it so it would look like you were dumping him. That was harder, imitating your handwriting.

Faith's entire body was shaking. She could hardly believe this. How could Blaine be so underhanded and sneaky? How could he lie and deceive her about the most important thing in her life, all for his own gain? How could he ruin almost ten years of her life? In those ten years, she'd found things to be happy about, relying on her faith and her love for her family to get her through, but the time apart from Jag had been torture. She'd ached for Jag, but she'd also been ticked at him for dumping her so coldly. Blaine had claimed to love her, but this wasn't love. It was manipulation, and it was horrible.

I'm so sorry, Faith. I know you'll be furious, and I don't blame you. My only excuse is that I was an eighteen-year-old kid in love with the most beautiful angel I'd ever known, and I knew I didn't have a chance of winning you away from Jag. As the years went by, I talked myself into believing I'd done the best thing for you, you wouldn't have liked leaving the valley or dealing with Jag's famous lifestyle, and I was much more devoted to you than he could ever be. I pushed what I'd done from my mind and focused on what I was meant to do: love you. I pray you'll forgive me, and I pray you'll know that I did love you with all my heart. This past year has been the happiest, most amazing time, far better than I had even dreamt it could be, being close to you and loving you. I'd be nothing without you. I adore you.

Love forever,

Blaine

Faith realized she was tearing the edges of the letter from holding it so tightly. She forced herself to release her grip, jam it back in the envelope, and stomp her way through the snow back to the car. All she wanted was to be warm and safe. Tears slid down her face. She'd trusted Blaine and committed herself to him because he loved her so much. Instead, he had betrayed her.

Maybe she could understand the teenage kid scheming up the letter-switching and breaking up his two friends so he could be with the girl he wanted. Yet they'd been close friends all those years, she'd dated him during his breaks from college and more seriously after he graduated from law school, and she had let him talk her into marrying him. At some point, she would've thought the mature, even-keeled, kind Blaine would've wanted to rectify his mistake. He hadn't even wanted her to know what he'd done before he died. He'd wanted her to wait a year.

Her mind was scrambling and twisting, and her entire body felt both numb and in pain at the same time. She slid into the car, twisted the key, and then just sat there as the car warmed up. Her head settled against the headrest. She didn't want to go home. She didn't want to be around the memories of Blaine. Not right now. She knew he'd loved her, in his own twisted way, but a love based on deception like this wasn't really love and for sure wasn't a healthy relationship. Not that they'd ever had a healthy relationship as she'd always tried to bury deep the fact that she was still in love with Jag.

Jag. He'd claimed she'd broken his heart. Oh my! She put a hand over her mouth, and her stomach pitched. He *would* believe she broke his heart; Blaine had rewritten their letters, so Jag got dumped just like she did. Resolve and vengeance rushed through her. Blaine had done all this because he'd talked himself into believing it was better for her. What about her chances for love with Jag, the man she'd always longed for? Blaine's love was selfish, only focused on what he wanted. Jag deserved to know the truth. He deserved to know it right now.

Jamming the car into gear, she hurried out of the cemetery and down the side road until she got to the main road that headed out of the valley. She had to find Jag, and she had to tell him the truth. Who knew what would happen then? A swarm of butterflies invaded her stomach. If she knew Jag at all, he wouldn't hesitate to show her exactly how much he cared. Excitement filled her entire body. She was done feeling guilty about what she'd assumed was misplaced love for Jag. Her feelings for him were pure and right, and she'd known that inside all along. That was why she'd never been able to let him go. Now if only her old car would drive faster so she could find him.

F aith hurried up the steps and into the main lodge of the ski resort. It was beautiful with windows overlooking the valley and the resort. There were a myriad of Christmas decorations brightening the place, as well as several smaller trees and one grand tree tall enough to reach the open section of the second story.

She hurried to the front desk girl. "Hi. I'm Faith Gra— ... Summers." She was dumping that last name now. Hot anger was still tracing through her at Blaine's deception. She wasn't sure how he could've lived with himself, lived with the lies, for so many years. "I need to know what room Jag Parros is staying in."

The girl's neatly penciled eyebrows rose. "I can't tell you that, ma'am."

"I work here. In the spa." Faith tilted her head and forced a smile. "So you can tell me."

"No, I can't."

Faith's frustration was already boiling just under the surface, and she was likely to explode. "You can, and you will." She leaned closer and wondered if she looked threatening enough, because she definitely should. She'd watched enough hockey to know how to win in a fight. "Call Gavin Strong. Ask your boss if you should give me the room number."

The girl blinked quickly. "I'm not bothering Mr. Strong. He's with his family today."

"Call him," Faith said; her voice was almost taunting. "If you don't, he'll fire you for not helping me." She jutted out her chin, praying it was true. Heath and Nick Strong were a year older and younger than her, respectively, and she didn't know the oldest brother, Gavin, that well. He seemed like a nice guy, though, and she hoped she wasn't the one who'd get fired for this. She loved her job and the spa.

The girl stared at her, as if calling her bluff. Finally, she muttered. "I won't do it. I will not bother Mr. Strong, and I will not give out guest information to anyone, unless you have a warrant or are a police officer."

Faith's determination leaked out. She felt like she'd been wrung through the spin cycle today, and now, when she finally knew the truth and knew what she wanted, she couldn't find Jag. Her heart cried for him.

She leaned heavily against the desk and couldn't fight it when tears slowly pricked at her eyelids and then traced down her cheeks. Luckily, no one was waiting behind her for the front desk, but there were people coming in and out of the front door, the restaurant, and down the stairs or out of the elevator. She glanced around for that redhead reporter but couldn't see her. Wouldn't the woman love this?

"Please," Faith murmured, staring into the girl's blue eyes. "I've had the worst day you can imagine. My husband died a year ago."

"Oh, I am sorry."

"Thank you." She took a deep breath. As little as she wanted to share this with some stranger, she knew she needed something convincing or she would never get past this very disciplined gate-keeper. "He left me a letter to read. It explained how ten years ago he'd kept me from the man I love … Jag Parros." She sniffled and blinked quickly.

The girl's gaze was slowly growing more compassionate.

"Ten long years I've loved Jag, and because of deception from the man I ended up marrying, I've been kept from the man I was supposed to be with. Now I know the truth and all I want to do is find Jag, tell him the truth, and hold him close again." She lifted her clasped hands, beseeching the girl with her eyes. "Please, just a room number. I promise he will want to see me, and you won't get in trouble."

The girl leaned toward her and nodded, and Faith's heart leapt. Finally, she was going to get the number, and then she was going to find Jag. She would hand him the letter. Then she would wait for that change in his eyes, the comprehension, the love for her taking over. Then he'd sweep her off her feet, kiss her, and they'd start off where they'd picked up.

"I can't give you his room number," the girl whispered.

Faith's shoulders rounded, and more traitorous tears rolled out.

"I'm sorry. But I can try to call his room for you."

Faith would rather see him in person, but it was better than nothing. She nodded. "Please."

The girl smiled, checked her computer, and then, shielding the phone as if Faith could crane her neck and get the room number, she quickly dialed the number. She kept her bright smile focused on Faith, but then her smile slowly drooped as the phone rang and no one picked up. She couldn't quite meet Faith's gaze as she set the phone back down and said, "I can leave a note for him from you."

Faith looked around the main floor of the lodge. It was busy, but not overwhelming so. She pointed to a leather couch set by the fire. "Thank you." She tried to compose herself. "Please leave a note for Jag Parros that Faith Summers needs to speak to him. I'll be waiting right over there."

The girl nodded quickly. "Thank you, ma'am."

Faith walked wearily away. Jag. She just wanted to find him, be with him. Wasn't ten years long enough to be apart? She sank onto the couch. Her stomach rumbled at the delicious scent of steak and fresh-baked bread coming from the restaurant. She pulled out her phone to check the time; it was only six-thirty. Jag could be at one of the restaurants downtown, or he could be at the restaurant right here. Maybe she'd just peek and hope that a miracle was still in store for her.

CHAPTER SIX

J ag was probably acting off with his family. He couldn't keep going like this. He needed Faith, and he needed her now. He wanted to respect that it was the anniversary of Blaine's death and she needed to mourn, but deep inside he could hardly stand the fact that she'd ever been with Blaine. It just wasn't right. Despite all the junk and years that were between them now, Faith and Jag fit. They'd always fit. Like their gloves on the glass, nothing could come between them. She'd dumped him in that letter, but after being around her now, he realized he should've chased after her years ago, talked it out, and not let it come between them.

The family was sitting down to dinner at the beautiful resort restaurant, where the windows faced the ski slopes. The restaurant was crowded and busy. The waitress brought their drinks and was waiting now for their orders. Everyone else had ordered, and all were looking expectantly at Jag. He glanced up at the waitress, but a movement from behind her caught his eye.

Leaning around the waitress, he whispered, "Faith." She was tentatively walking through the restaurant, looking around at tables as if searching for someone. Her face looked tear-stained, and her eyes were anxious. Her gaze kept darting around. She leaned forward, and then disappointment filled her face as if she hadn't seen who she was hoping for.

Jag wanted to stand and shout that he was here. She had to be looking for him, but his legs were suddenly shaky and unsteady. Was Faith coming for him or was he in for another disappointment? He didn't know if he could recover from anymore rejection.

Her gaze finally landed on him, and she lit up, smiling so big her dimple came out. Jag's heart threatened to burst. Her loving look made it clear that nothing could come between them.

"Sir?" the waitress asked.

Jag felt a burst of energy and stood, hurried around the waitress, and rushed to Faith. He wanted to swing her off her feet and then kiss her until they had to come up for air, but a small part of him recognized that she must be going through something horrible since it was Blaine's death day; the redness of her eyes was a giveaway. She'd left Jag standing in that parking lot a couple of hours ago and not been happy with him at all. Why had she come for him now?

"Jag." She stared up at him with a gaze that reminded him of their teenage years, when she'd adored him and wanted to spend every minute next to him. "We need to talk. We *really* need to talk."

Jag nodded. He'd talk until he was blue if it meant another chance with Faith. They could work out all the garbage between them. They had to.

"Jag?" his dad's voice asked from behind. "Is everything okay?"

His family. He turned back. "Yes. Faith's going to join us for dinner." He looked back at her.

She smiled, though he could tell that she really didn't want to put off whatever she wanted to talk about. He didn't either, but he hated to just rush out on his family. Jag took her arm and walked her over to the table.

"Faith!" his mom and Brielle squealed at the same time. They both jumped up and hugged her, gushing over her, wanting to know everything she'd been up to the past ten years.

They paused to let the waitress take her and Jag's orders, and Faith shook her dad's hand and was introduced to Mason, but then the women were pumping her with questions again. Jag studied her. She looked drained, and yet every time she met his gaze, she sparkled. Was that just wishful thinking on his part? He noticed she left mention of her marriage to Blaine out of the conversation completely. Was that because she thought it would be uncomfortable or hurt them, or did she want to forget the memories of Blaine? That was selfish of him to think, but he wanted to pick up where they'd left off ten years ago and push Blaine from her memory.

F aith enjoyed being around Jag's family again and was able to get some of the delicious pasta down, even though her stomach was rolling. She kept glancing at Jag, and her heart threatened to burst. He was right here, he hadn't dumped her, and she still loved him. Did he love her back? The look in his blue eyes seemed to say so, and over the past two days, he'd chased her pretty hard. Had he only chased her to get answers, or did he still feel the special connection between them that had always been there?

The dinner was fun, but finally it ended. They all stood and walked out into the open area of the lodge. His sister, Brielle, who Faith had always adored, said slyly, "I'm guessing you two want some time alone?"

Faith gazed up at him. She definitely wanted some time alone. Where to go, though? She didn't want to go outside and freeze, but she didn't want to suggest they go up to his room, and she really didn't want to take him back to her house.

"Yes, we do," Jag murmured, slipping his arm around her back.

Faith's heart walloped in her chest as his warm arm held her against his side. How would it feel to kiss him again? After ten years of fasting from Jag's touch and kiss, she needed a lot of time alone with him. First she had to share the letter and talk through all the pain, though. "Would you want ... a tour of the spa?" That would be a good spot. They could sit in the back therapy room, in their own chairs, and talk. Snuggling together sounded like more fun, but she definitely wouldn't be getting any talking done then.

Jag's eyebrows lifted. "Sure."

He was probably confused how she could be so hot and cold with him, but soon she could explain and hopefully kiss him good and long.

His family said their goodbyes and started walking toward the elevator. The reporter, Sheryl, came from behind Faith and strode up to Jag's mom. "Are you just thrilled about Jag's recent engagement?" she asked.

His mom looked at the woman in confusion. "Excuse me?"

Sheryl's smile became positively wicked. "Did you not know that Jag Parros is engaged to Faith Grainger? It's beautiful that she could move on from her husband's death so quickly."

His mom was still looking a step behind, and Faith didn't blame her. Faith wasn't sure why Jag needed to pretend to be engaged to her, and she wished it could be real, but she instinctively didn't want to give Sheryl any ammo.

"My husband has been gone for a year," Faith spoke up. "And being engaged to Jag is the happiest I have *ever* been."

Jag's mom gave her a soft smile. "We're thrilled as well, sweetheart."

Brielle gave the reporter a contemptuous look. "All of us can hardly wait to have Faith in the family. And who are you?" She looked down her nose at her, and Faith had to hide a laugh.

"I'm an independently contracted reporter," Sheryl said, all mightier-than-thou.

"You look it," Brielle said snidely. "Faith, Jag, let's go upstairs and chat in our suite."

Jag directed Faith past Sheryl, who was shooting daggers at the entire family. They got into the elevator, and nobody said anything as it ascended. The silence was uncomfortable, and Faith wondered if his family was upset at her for not telling them she'd been married, upset at Jag for lying about being engaged, or just upset at Sheryl for being a piece of work.

They arrived at the sixth floor and walked down the hall. Mason pulled out a key, opened the door, and held it for all of them. Faith was temporarily distracted from her worries about her conversation with his family and her need to get Jag alone, as she drank in the sight of this gorgeous suite. She'd heard the sixth floor was incredible, but this was beyond what she'd expected. The suite was two stories, boasting a spacious living room and kitchen area with a balcony-type railing overlooking them from above. She assumed the bedroom portion was upstairs. The floor-to-ceiling windows gave an incredible view of the mountain to the north and the ski resort, which was lit up for night skiing. She guessed it was one-way glass like her spa. A beautifully deco-rated Christmas tree towered in the corner, and there were even stockings hanging on the lit fireplace.

Brielle gestured to the couches. "I can't wait to hear this story," she said.

"Me either," Jag's mom said.

They all settled onto the couches. Jag gave Faith a longing look, and she knew exactly how he felt. She was more than ready to tell him everything and kiss him good and long, but he obviously had something important to tell his family.

Jag spread his hands. "Sheryl is a vicious reporter who has it in for me. She followed me here to try to substantiate rumors that I threw the Islanders game."

"No brother of mine would throw a game, especially against the Islanders," Brielle said with disgust.

Mason nodded. "For sure. We'd kick you out of the family."

Jag's dad smiled at that, but then he sobered. "What's really going on, son?"

Jag looked to Faith. Everything was uncertain between them, and she hadn't even been able to tell him the truth about the letters and Blaine. He seemed to be deciding whether he still trusted her enough to share something. She stared into his blue eyes and willed him to believe that she adored him and would never betray him.

Jag wrapped his hand around hers, and her heart leapt. He took a deep breath and said, "My contract's up for renewal after this season. I know I've got a lot more years in me. My agent asked me to come here and try to get some good publicity. Little did I know that Sheryl would follow me in hopes of making me look even worse." He squeezed Faith's hand, smiling. "I lied and said I was engaged to Faith. I figured being engaged to her would be the best publicity I could get."

Brielle winked. "Definitely would up your stock, bro."

"Just like you do mine," Mason said, tugging her close and tenderly kissing her on the forehead.

Faith loved that they were so cute, but she sensed something else was going on with Jag. He was an unreal hockey player. Why would he need more good publicity?

Jag's mom smiled at Mason and Brielle, but then she turned to Jag. "Why be fake engaged? Let's do this for real."

Faith's heart started pumping hard and fast.

Jag looked down at her with as much tenderness as Mason had just looked at Brielle. "I would love to, but Faith and I have some things to work out."

"I want to work them out, though," she managed to squeak through her constricted throat. She didn't want to do this in front of his family, but she definitely wanted to talk. Now.

They stared at each other until Jag's dad broke the connection. "We'd be thrilled to have you in the family, Faith. I want to let you two go work those things out, but there's something else, son. You didn't look like yourself in that game against the Islanders. Are you injured and trying to hide that?"

Jag's hand tightened around hers. She leaned closer to him, trying to relay her support. Whatever was going on, she and his family would be here.

He looked around at everyone, and she followed his gaze. His mom and dad, Brielle, and Mason all looked concerned and interested. Faith had never felt as comfortable with Blaine's family as she did with Jag's family. There was so much love in this room.

"I was actually diagnosed with the flu after," Jag admitted. "That's why I felt so weak and had to pull myself from that game, but when I went in to the doctor and they ran a bunch of tests." He swallowed and then pushed out, "They discovered I have multiple sclerosis."

The room was quiet for half a beat, and then Brielle exploded. "No!" she cried out. "You've always been healthy and strong and ... no!" Mason pulled her close, and she buried her head in his chest.

Faith couldn't speak. She was clinging to Jag's hand every bit as fiercely as he was clinging to hers. Multiple sclerosis? Jag? When she stared at him, he looked to be the picture of health, but the debilitating disease picked and chose whoever it wanted. Her body hurt just thinking about him having to deal with this. Would his strength deteriorate? Would he be in a wheelchair? What would his future look like now?

His mom didn't say anything, but tears streamed down her pretty face. His dad pulled his mom close and looked to Jag, asking, "What are your doctors saying?"

"The prognosis is really hopeful. They said the symptoms are usually slow to progress. I mean, they can't guarantee it, and some people deteriorate quickly or in stops and starts, but with the right treatment, they're really hopeful that we can delay the symptoms for years and I can live a full life. I might eventually be in a wheelchair, but some have avoided that. There's no cure, but there are a lot of ideas to try, alternative treatments and therapies, and a specialized diet can sometimes help." He shrugged, but his eyes betrayed how concerned he was, maybe even scared.

Faith had never seen him look anything but strong and confident. She wouldn't blame him if he dissolved into a puddle of tears.

"Honestly, the doctors are really encouraging. They believe my progression will be slow, especially with staying on top of treatments. I haven't been that focused on the disease, more trying to keep it from the media, coaches, and owner, so I can renew my contract and keep playing."

"But son ..." His dad shook his head. "This is not something you can just work harder at and get rid of. Maybe you should look at giving up hockey."

"Give up hockey?" Jag stared at him as if he'd grown two heads. "No. I've got the best doctors in the nation. They're going to help me fight it, delay the progress, and I'm going to keep playing."

Faith loved his determination, but she had to know. "Is intense exercise recommended for someone with this disease?"

Jag kind of glowered down at her. He'd never get outright upset at her, but he didn't like her question. "Not really, but you know I'm not the average human." He forced a smile, winking at her.

"Jag." His mom's voice was soft and concerned. "Will you promise me to listen to the doctors?"

Jag nodded quickly. "I promise. I know it's a little unconventional, a hockey star with multiple sclerosis, but I feel like I can fight this, prolong the symptoms manifesting themselves, and still be successful at hockey for at least a few more years." He looked around and said quietly, "Can you support me in this and not tell anyone?"

Mason nodded decisively. "Of course, man."

Brielle's eyes were full of sadness, but she whispered, "You know we will."

"As long as you listen if the doctors tell you to stop playing," his dad said.

"I will." It sounded like Jag had to force out those words. Faith couldn't imagine how hard that was.

His mom stood and rushed across the small space. Jag released Faith's hand, stood, and opened his arms. He held his mother close as she cried. The room was otherwise silent.

Faith should've felt like an outsider, but she didn't. She could hear Jag murmuring to his mom, "It's going to be okay. It's going to be okay."

She wondered if he was trying to reassure himself as well. She remembered how terrifying it had been for Blaine when he'd been diagnosed with the brain tumor. This was very different, as Jag could potentially live a long life, but it was still scary to wonder what was coming and if he would end up weak and in a wheelchair. As she looked up at his strong body, embracing his much smaller mother, she could not even imagine him weak.

His mom finally pulled back and wiped at her eyes. She glanced down at Faith. "Are you okay, sweetheart?"

Faith put a hand on her heart. "Me? I'm just worried about Jag and all of you."

His mom eyed her perceptively. "This might change your future too."

Jag squeezed his mom and said, "I've got to talk her into marrying me before we ruin her future with her husband having a stupid disease."

"You all know how much work he's got cut out if he thinks he's talking me into marrying him," Faith said, faking sass. The letter. Soon it would be time to share it with him. How would he react? He was already dealing with so much.

Everyone laughed in relief. Jag looked around at his family. "I think that's my cue to get her alone and do some serious talking."

"Don't let your devoted family, who all adore you, keep you. All you want to do is get in some serious kissing," Brielle flung at him.

Jag pumped his eyebrows. "Smart sister I've got."

Faith's stomach was tumbling with excitement and nerves. She was still processing this disease Jag was dealing with, but now it was time to share the truth with him about Blaine and the letters. Some serious kissing would hopefully follow.

They all stood, and Jag took his time hugging each of his family members, lingering in embracing his mom. Faith gave them each a quick hug, and then Jag took her hand and led her from the room. The meaningful look in his eyes as he walked her across the hall to what must've been his suite was exciting, unnerving, and terrifying. They were finally going to talk. She was more than ready. If only she could anticipate how Jag would respond.

CHAPTER SEVEN

J ag couldn't believe it. He felt better than he had since before the diagnosis. No, better than he'd felt since he'd left Lonepeak Valley and this incredible woman ten years ago. She'd come for him, on Blaine's death day, no less. She'd held his hand as he shared the horrific news with his family. He pushed the diagnosis and his uncertain future from his mind. All that mattered to him was Faith. Would she want to be with him, knowing he might degenerate? Could they put the pain behind them and be together? She seemed open to talking about being engaged for real.

He loved his mom for bringing that up. He'd hugged her and tried to comfort her after sharing his news, while in reality she was the one comforting him like she'd always done, making him feel like he was ten again.

His entire family had taken the news much better than he'd expected. Brielle had exploded, but that was normal for Brielle.

She'd calmed down quickly. He didn't love that he'd promised he'd quit hockey if it was causing the disease to progress, but his doctors had been encouraging so far. He was in amazing shape, it was an illness with an unknown progression, and he could prolong the symptoms. He tried not to look too far into the future, what being weak and wheelchair-bound might do to him, but the thought of having Faith by his side gave him strength. If he could talk her into it.

They walked into his room. The maid service had left low lights on above the cabinets, and the Christmas tree sparkled in the corner. His suite was on the valley side, and the view was incredible during the day. Right now, the parking lot was glowing below them and he could see lights scattered throughout the small valley, concentrated along the main street.

He didn't turn on the overhead lights, preferring the more romantic lighting and hoping he could convince Faith to talk everything through and give him a chance. He'd forgive her for writing him off, and for marrying Blaine, of course he would.

They settled side by side on the couch. He turned slightly toward her and let his eyes trail over her beautiful face, those dark eyes that he loved, the slightly upturned nose, the smooth skin, and her firm jaw. His eyes lingered on her full lips, and he forced himself to meet her gaze again. The lips would come later. He hoped.

"Faith, I ..." He shook his head. "I want you to know that I forgive you for writing me off. I would always forgi—"

"Jag," she interrupted him. "Thank you for being willing to

forgive me, but I have to share something with you before you say anything else."

He stopped and nodded, but the too-serious look in her eyes was scaring him a little bit. Was there something besides her Dear John letter and marrying his former best friend between them? He already had enough to deal with, battling this disease and fighting to keep performing as a renowned hockey star. Yet all of that faded in the background as he stared at her and waited for what she was going to say. He'd love her no matter what, and he was coming to this with his own baggage. It wasn't going to be easy for her if she committed to love him and he got weak and maybe died prematurely.

Faith studied him for half a beat, as if gauging how he was going to take whatever she needed to share. "Blaine wrote me a letter when he was diagnosed."

Oh, great. He didn't really want to focus on Blaine right now.

Her pretty mouth pursed. "He asked me to wait until today, the year anniversary, to read it." She pulled the letter out of her purse, and for a second looked like she wanted to hand it to him, but then she shoved it back in and took a shuddering breath.

Jag took her hands in his. He didn't want to read Blaine's words anyway. She could paraphrase, and then whatever was between them could work out. "Faith, it's okay. Whatever it is, it's okay."

"Thank you." Her eyes looked suspiciously bright, but she didn't cry. She sighed and then said quickly, "Blaine tricked us both."

Jag tilted his head. "How?"

"He stole the letters you sent me from school, altered one, and made it look like you dumped me to pursue your career in hockey."

Jag's eyes widened as his stomach dropped out. "How ... how dare he?"

She nodded. "He also intercepted my letters to you; then he took the one I wrote after you dumped me—I mean, I thought you dumped me—and altered it as well. I'd assume he made it look like I'd received your earlier letters and I was choosing to dump you first."

Jag could hardly comprehend this. He stared at her for a few seconds, and then he stood and paced to the windows and back again a few times. Blaine had been his best friend back in the day, yet Blaine had betrayed him and then had the nerve to pursue and marry Faith.

He looked back at her. She was shifting uncomfortably. Jag was angry, but he was more concerned about how Faith was taking this. "He betrayed us both and then talked you into marrying him?"

"Yes. He worked on me for years. Every break he had from college, he'd come see me. He texted me and called me nonstop while he was away. I thought he was my best friend. He was very devoted to me, and he always said he loved me enough for the both of us." She shook her head. "I'm so ticked at him right now. That's probably why he asked me to wait a year, so I wouldn't dig up his grave and spit on him."

Jag let out a surprised grunt of a laugh, trying to process this. As it sank in, he could understand her anger, and he felt plenty of his own for what Blaine had robbed them of, but overriding that was the compassion for Faith. She'd fallen victim to the vicious ploy of an obviously twisted mind, and she had married the guy, had given herself to him. It made Jag nauseous. "I'm so sorry. I can't imagine what you're going through right now." He shook his head and realized he wasn't innocent of piling heavy issues on her. "And then I load more on sharing about my disease."

"Oh, Jag." She stood quickly and walked to him. Putting a hand on his arm, she stared up at him, so sweet and beautiful. "I want to be there for you. Thank you for trusting me enough to include me in that."

Jag got a little choked up. He'd forgotten how pure and incredible she was. How he loved her. "Thank you, Faith. Thank you for being here." He tenderly cupped her chin with his palm. As they stared at each other, Jag's mind shifted, and a stream of happiness rushed through him like he was sending a puck straight past two defenders and the goalie into the net. "Do you realize what this means?"

She gave him a questioning look. "I married a scumbag?"

Jag couldn't help but laugh again. "No. I mean, yes, I'm sorry that he tricked you like that, but Faith ... All these years, I longed for you and I wanted to forget that horrible letter I thought you sent and come for you. I kept myself busy with hockey and talked myself into believing that you truly didn't want me, but none of that is true." He felt all lit up inside. "You still adore me and want to be with me."

Faith laughed. "Now that is for sure."

Jag whooped, picked her up off the ground, and swung her around. "Finally, Faith, we can be together again. If you had any clue how I've missed you, ached for you all these years ..." He set her on her feet, released her waist, and held up his hands. She grinned so big her dimple showed as she matched her hands to his. "Nothing can come between us," he whispered softly.

"Nothing."

Their hands twined together, symbolic of the past behind them and the future in front of them.

Faith released his hands and rested her hands on his arms. He took this as his cue. He cupped her face with his hands. She wrapped her hands more tightly around his biceps, clinging to him and smiling so sweetly yet sassily up at him. "How about you give me a long demonstration of how much you've missed me?"

"Yes, ma'am." Jag didn't need to be told twice. He bent down and softly pressed his lips to hers. Warmth and joy spread quickly from her into him. Faith let out the cutest little moan, and Jag couldn't hold back any longer. He ran his hands down to her lower back and pulled her as tight to him as he could, and then he proceeded to show her exactly how much he'd missed her with his kiss.

Happiness like this could only exist with her. Jag was exactly where he'd wanted to be for ten years.

***

Faith ran her hands up Jag's shoulders and wrapped them tightly around his neck. His lips lit up her world, as hot and beautiful as a roaring fire. She returned his kiss with all the passion and longing she'd locked inside of her for ten years. No man's kiss had ever warmed her up like Jag's did, and she knew inherently as he took possession of her mouth and her heart that Jag was her missing piece and she was complete in his arms.

She caught a breath and stared up into his handsome face. Even though she was ecstatic, a part of her was still furious at Blaine. He'd robbed them of ten years, and now with Jag's prognosis ... What if it progressed rapidly and she lost him? She hugged him fiercely, burying her face in his neck as tears pricked at her eyelids.

Jag held her close, but after a little while he pulled back and smiled down at her. "Where were we ... Faith?" He stared at her. "Why are you crying, love?"

She blinked and wiped the tears away. "I just want you close. What if something happens to you?"

"Is it too much to ask of you? Loving me when I might be ..." He swallowed and then muttered, "Disabled soon?"

"No!" She shook her head, holding him tighter. "No. I'd love you if you were going to die tomorrow or be in a coma for life. Nothing will stop me loving you."

Jag smiled tenderly at her. "Thank you."

"Nothing has stopped me from loving you, Jag. Even when I was married to Blaine."

He winced as if he could hardly stand to hear the words, "married to Blaine".

"I felt so guilty because I still just adored you. Even though I thought you'd written me off and gone on to success without me, I always loved you and longed to be with you. Only you."

Jag kissed her softly. "I was the same. I tried to date, tried to find someone to replace you."

Now she was the one wincing.

Jag smiled. "But there's no one like you, Faith. No one for me but you."

"Don't you forget it," she teased.

He lifted her off the ground, hugging her tight. Giving her a lingering kiss, he tugged her over to the couch, settled down, and pulled her onto his lap. "Can we just be close? Talk the night away? I want to know everything about you, everything I've missed that you want to share."

She doubted he wanted to hear everything, as much of her last ten years had been centered on Blaine, but there was a lot she could share.

"So you just want to talk?" She pumped her eyebrows, and then she leaned close and kissed that scar next to his lip.

Jag groaned and turned his head to hers, murmuring against her lips. "You're right. Talking is highly overrated."

Faith opened her mouth to protest, but he was already kissing her. There was no world where she could protest that. She cuddled against him and let him take full advantage of her mouth. He was right. They could talk anytime. Happiness like this was meant to be savored.

CHAPTER EIGHT

J ag followed Faith home late that night to make sure she got home safe. He gave her a lingering kiss on the doorstep but didn't come in. He'd teased about talking or kissing the night away, but they both knew that was playing with fire. They'd waited this long to be together; they could wait until they were married. Married? There'd been the talk about being fake engaged and real engaged, but she wondered when they'd officially make that next step. They lived on different sides of the country, and both of their lives would need some adjustments if they got married. She'd do anything to be with Jag, but the thought of leaving her valley and her family, her safety net, was unsettling. She'd left for short vacations and that had been fine, but to permanently leave everything she knew and loved? Only for Jag would she consider it.

The next morning, she awoke to the ringing of the doorbell, then a rapping on her front door. She groaned and peeled open her eyes. The sun wasn't even up. She glanced at her phone. Seven-ten. She only had time in her schedule to sleep in on Saturdays, but it was Christmas Eve and she and Jag had been up really late last night.

She hurried out of bed and rushed through the house to the front door. Looking through the peephole, she grinned. Jag was standing there, shifting his weight from foot to foot. He lifted his hand to knock again. Faith yanked the door open, and he stumbled forward. He recovered quickly and laughed. "Good morning."

"Good would have been ten. Come in, it's freezing." She hugged herself for warmth, only in a tank top and shorts.

Jag stepped in, and she shut the door behind him. He took off his coat and set it on the bench in the entryway. He wasn't even looking at the house; he was hyper-focused on her. His eyes slowly roved over her body and then met her gaze. "Do you dress like this all the time?" he asked.

Faith patted at her hair; she probably looked a wreck. "I was asleep," she protested.

Jag swallowed hard, and the look in his eyes brought warmth to her abdomen. "You ... sleep like that?"

"Yes, I sleep like this."

He tilted his head. "And you answer the door like that?"

She grunted and rolled her eyes. "I saw it was you."

"What if I had been the FedEx driver?"

She pumped her eyebrows. "Oh, then I would've planted a big kiss on him."

Jag growled low in his throat and stepped in closer. He looked incredible in a nicely fitted white long-sleeved shirt and black jogger-style pants. "You'd better only answer the door like this for me."

"Jealous much?" Faith laughed and pushed at his shoulder.

Jag grabbed her hand and tugged her close. "You have no idea." He spun her around, pressed her back into the door, and bent down low. His lips grazed her bare shoulder, and the warmth she'd been feeling became an inferno.

She moaned softly, and his gaze darted up to hers; his blue eyes so taken with her that she could hardly stand up straight. Thankfully he had her pinned against the door and she didn't have to do anything but enjoy his touch. He trailed his lips slowly, achingly across her shoulder, up the side of her neck, and to her ear. He whispered softly in her ear, "No one sees this but me."

Faith loved the possessive note in his voice and she absolutely agreed. She wanted no man but Jag. "Ask me nicely," she breathed, as his strong body pinned her in place and his lips made their way closer and closer to her mouth.

Jag grinned and captured her lips with his. The kiss was powerful and seductive and had her panting for air. He pulled back, and she tried to form coherent thoughts. She wanted to keep teasing with him, so she said again, "I thought you were going to ask me nicely."

Jag framed her face with his hands, tilted her head, and said, "I just did."

Faith laughed. "You'd better ask again."

"Yes, ma'am." Then he was kissing her, and all rational thought disappeared.

Jag got permission to take Faith skating on the Strongs' lake, which was a couple miles east of their house. They said hello to Gavin and one of the twins—Jag thought it was Ella—then hiked along the snow-covered trail to the lake. Jag carried their skates and happily followed Faith up the trail, and they chatted like they'd never missed a moment of being together. The trail was well packed, so they didn't even need the snowshoes Gavin had offered for them to use.

When they got to the lake, Jag felt like he had the entire world in his palm. He loved this spot as much as any in the world. They put their skates on, and Jag tugged her out onto the ice. They skated along more slowly than he normally did, holding hands and sneaking glances and smiles. It had about killed him earlier to let her go and get ready. Seeing her in only a tank top and shorts had him envisioning married life much too quickly. Could he talk her into marrying him really, really soon? Would she be okay relocating? He loved this valley and would happily stay here anytime they could, but his home for the foreseeable future was Boston—as long as nobody found out about his degenerative condition and he got another contract after this season.

"When do you have to go back?" Faith asked. They'd decided to just be together this morning and then spend the afternoon with his family and the evening with hers. Already they felt like a couple, and he loved it.

"I have practice on the twenty-sixth and a game on the twenty-seventh."

Her face fell, but she squeezed his gloved hand as if she was fine. He'd always loved Faith's strength and resilience. She'd stayed much the same as he remembered her from before, but there was a maturity and depth to her that had increased.

"Will you come with me?" he asked.

Faith tilted her head as they glided along on the ice. "I have to work."

Jag turned around and skated backwards, grasping both of her hands. "Faith, if we're going to be together ... Are you all right finding a job in Boston?"

"Boston?" Her brow furrowed. "You want me to move to Boston?"

Jag chuckled, but it was uneasy. He glided to a stop and held on to her hands. "It's kind of better for a married couple to live in the same city."

Faith just stared at him. She was stalling, and he was suddenly afraid that she wasn't at all ready to move and be with him. "I know you claimed a fake engagement for the reporter lady," she said, "but are you ready ... for us to be together?"

Jag understood now. She was as vulnerable and uncertain as he was. He hastened to reassure her, "Being with you is all I can think about. Nothing about what I feel for you could be fake. I don't have a ring yet, but I'll get one and I'll ask you in some big way." He tugged her close, wishing they didn't have the coats between them but at the same time grateful they did. She made him want to be married right now. "I can't be without you again." Staring down into her deep brown eyes, he begged, "Please say you feel the same."

Faith lifted her face up to him. She couldn't go on tiptoes with her skates on, but Jag happily obliged her by bending down and kissing her long and good. When he pulled back, she didn't answer as quickly as he'd like. "I don't want to pressure you or uproot your life," he said into the silence, "but I need you with me. Can we make this work?"

Faith got a teasing glint in her eyes. "You know you haven't really told me you love me."

His eyes widened. "I love you, Faith Summers. I adore you. I worship you. I will do anything in the world to have you be mine."

She smiled. "I guess that'll have to do, until you learn how to be a little gushy for me."

Jag chuckled and bent down close again. "I'll show you gush."

She winked up at him. "I can't wait," she said just before they kissed.

In the back of his mind, Jag knew that she hadn't really agreed to move to Boston, but that would work out. They loved each other. They were going to get officially engaged soon. Now if only he could bring her home with him in two days. The vision of seeing her in his box at the next Bruins game wearing his jersey was only upstaged by the vision of them married and her only wearing that tank top and shorts. He increased the pressure of the kiss. Okay, the vision of them married was definitely at the top.

CHAPTER NINE

Faith loved ice skating with Jag again, especially the kissing, but something in her was scared. She didn't know if she wanted to leave her little happy valley. Maybe it was pathetic, but she'd only left for vacations. She'd done high school, swim team, and then beauty school in the nearby town of Vail. She'd never moved away. She'd ached for Jag over the years, but she'd been happy here.

Glancing up at Jag as they hiked back down the trail from the lake, she felt a surge of love. He smiled down at her, and the surge intensified. She'd go anywhere, do anything for him. Putting him first was the right path for her.

"Do you want to do something fun?" she asked.

"Kiss you nonstop. Sure."

She giggled. "Okay, not quite as fun as that."

"Dang. Got my hopes up for nothing."

They were approaching the back of Gavin Strong's house.

"So what do you have in mind … that's not quite as fun as kissing you?"

She smiled, loving that he was so taken with her. Blaine had claimed he loved her desperately, but his love had felt oppressive and controlling. Jag's love felt invigorating and thrilling.

They went to walk around the house, not wanting to disturb the family, and Faith's boss, on Christmas Eve. Austin Strong, a cute ten-year-old boy, ran out onto the back patio. "Hey, pretty lady," he called. "Hey, my favorite hockey player, Jag Parros."

"Hi, Austin." Faith raised her hand. "Are you excited for Christmas?"

"For sure." He jogged up to them with a pencil and paper in hand. Staring up at Jag with hero worship, he said, "Can you sign this for me, Mr. Parros, sir?"

Faith smiled. He was adorable.

Jag grinned down at him, ruffled his golden-brown hair, and held out his hand. "For sure." He took the paper and pressed it against the side of the house to write a little note to Austin and then signed it.

Austin grasped it in his hands. "Thank you," he said breathlessly, "I hope Santa finds you." With that, he darted back into the house.

Gavin was waiting at the patio door for him and waved to them. "Thanks," he called.

"Thanks for letting us skate. Merry Christmas."

"Merry Christmas," he returned.

Gavin was a serious dude. He used to intimidate Faith a little bit when she was younger and hanging out with Nick, but she knew he was a good guy and he was a fabulous boss. He was really fair with all of his employees and gave generous Christmas bonuses, and she'd talked with numerous employees who he'd helped in different ways when they had family trouble or medical emergencies.

Jag walked her to his rented Audi, got her door, waited while she climbed in, and then set the skates in the back seat. Shutting her door, he walked around and settled in. "So maybe I'll just let you surprise me. Where to?"

She loved every moment spent with him. She glanced at the clock on the dashboard. It was eleven. "Well, we have two hours until lunch and the matinee movie with your family. What do you think about getting our swimsuits? There's an incredible room at the spa that has different heated pools, and one pool with jets will massage every part of your body, and then there's this bubble bed that you lie on and you think you're in heaven."

Jag was staring at her with rapt attention. "And I get to kiss you in each of these spots?"

She laughed. "I don't think you're going to want to kiss me in the cold plunge."

He winked. "Think again. There isn't a spot on earth I wouldn't want to be kissing you."

Faith couldn't help putting her hand to her heart and sighing.

She hated to think of what would happen on the twenty-sixth when he had to leave her, but she'd deal with that when it happened. Right now, she was going to enjoy every second.

F aith thought her idea was incredibly brilliant when Jag walked out of the spa's locker room wearing his swim trunks. He looked good with his tall, lean body and his sculpted chest, shoulders, and arms, but the light in his blue eyes and the grin on his face were much more appealing than his perfect physique. He might lose that muscle tone with his disease or age, but he would never lose the qualities that made him inherently perfect: his thoughtfulness, his fun sense of humor, his dedication to God and his family, his integrity, and his love for her.

He walked right up to her and gave her a quick kiss. "You're so beautiful," he murmured against her lips.

"So are you."

He grinned. "Thank you, thank you very much." He straightened and looked around at the myriad of pools. "Which one's the cold plunge?"

Faith pointed to the right, and Jag swooped her off her feet and into his arms. She instinctively wrapped her arms tight around his broad back. "What are you doing?" she asked, breathless from being close to him.

Jag's grin was almost wicked. He didn't answer her, just ran for the cold plunge pool.

Faith gasped out. "No, not yet. Let's get hot first."

"I'm already hot just being close to you, and I owe you one for the push into the pool." Jag winked at her, pumped up the steps, and then leapt in with her in his arms.

Faith screamed in delight. The cold water hit her like a wall. She gasped, and then her head went under. Jag was holding her tight, and her body felt like it was surrounded by ice. She tried to push her way out of his arms, but he held her close and stood easily, lifting her up. None of the pools in here were over five feet deep, so the average adult could safely touch the bottom.

She stood easily next to him, pressing against his muscular chest and shivering violently. "So cold." She tried to push him toward the stairs. "Hot tub, now."

"I have to kiss you in here first."

"Make it quick."

"Aw ..."

Faith pushed onto tiptoes and kissed him, hard. Pulling back, she said, "Let me out of here and I'll kiss you for as long as you want in the other pools."

Jag's grin grew. "Deal." He swept her into his arms again and pushed toward the stairs and out of the water.

"You don't have to carry me everywhere." She clung to his neck, loving being so close to him.

"Ah, but I do. If you could see how incredible you look in that swimsuit, you'd understand."

Faith smiled. "Thank you. I'd say it back, but it'd sound cheesy."

"I like cheesy." He carried her into the next pool and set her down in the almost too-hot water. Her toes and fingers tingled like crazy, but they adjusted quickly to the heat, much more quickly than they ever would to that cold.

Jag pulled her against his chest. The warm water surrounded them, but she liked his arms surrounding her even better. "Kiss for as long as I want?"

"Well, we do have that lunch appointment with your family."

He shrugged, and her mouth went dry as the muscle rippled under the smooth, tanned skin of his shoulders. "They love you. They won't complain if we're late."

Faith laughed, but he cut it off by pressing his lips to hers. She didn't mind; quite the contrary, she returned the kiss happily.

CHAPTER TEN

J ag thought this was the best Christmas of his life. After their unreal spa experience of kissing in every different pool and then almost falling asleep as they cuddled on the bubble beds, he and Faith had showered quickly and gone to lunch with his family. Brielle had teased them about their wet hair mercilessly, but all of his family was so happy to see them together, to see him happy, that they didn't seem to mind that they'd arrived late, causing everyone to miss the movie and end up playing a card game in his parents' suite instead.

They'd spent Christmas Eve with her family, and he loved the rambunctious crew. She had seven siblings, all younger, and they were a lot of fun. Only one of her sisters was married, and Jag really liked her husband, a pediatrician from Denver.

Jag hadn't seen or heard from Sheryl since yesterday, and he prayed she'd moved on to another story or maybe gone to see her own family for Christmas. Even nasty reporters like Sheryl should have a family who semi-liked them. She had put out some stories about his fiancée, not painting Faith in the best light, but not being outright slanderous either. Sheryl knew that line and walked it continuously, sharing stories that bordered on scandal and got the attention without being defamatory enough to warrant an actual lawsuit.

The situation annoyed him, and he considered having his agent and lawyer slap a lawsuit on her just to scare her. Nothing would scare Sheryl, though, and he didn't care if the world knew he was engaged to Faith. If only he'd had time to buy her a ring. He hadn't even had time to get her a Christmas present, and that bothered him a lot. When he somehow convinced her to fly to Boston with him on the twenty-sixth, he'd find a way to get her a whole bunch of presents, especially an engagement ring. Would she want to pick it out herself or have him choose? Hmm.

On Christmas Eve, he hated to leave her with only a kiss on her parents' doorstep and no serious talk of her committing to fly home with him in a day and a half, or how soon she would marry him. She'd been married before, and he hated to think about that, but maybe she wouldn't want the big, fancy wedding and year-long engagement. A long engagement would destroy him. The problem was that he was in season. Regular season went until April and playoffs went until June if you were in the running for the Cup. Unless she was willing to elope, they'd probably have to wait until June.

A snowstorm blew in on Christmas morning, and he woke up to an amazing view from his suite's windows of the picturesque valley down below. He didn't want to be without Faith, but they'd already pushed their moms by not spending every part of Christmas Eve with them. They decided to spend Christmas morning with their individual families, and then they'd have lunch with her family and dinner with his.

His mom had an entire Christmas breakfast, presents, and stockings in their suite. Jag, Brielle, and Mason tore through the presents like they were little kids. A knock came at the door, and his mom said, "That'll be breakfast."

"I'll get it." Jag lumbered to his feet and hurried across the large open room to the suite door. He swung it wide. The lady on the other side was familiar. She looked like she'd been through some hard times since high school, though.

"Jag?" Tracy grinned up at him. "Wow, it's good to see you." She gave him a quick hug and stepped back. "You look great, amazing. My son watches all your hockey games. I told him you were my friend in high school, and he thought that was amazing."

"Thanks." He didn't know how to tell her she looked great, because she looked exhausted. He felt sick that she was working on Christmas morning instead of being with her son. "What's your son's name?"

"Josh." Her smile got bigger, making her look more like the Tracy he remembered. "He's seven and absolutely hilarious."

Jag almost expressed his condolences that she wasn't with him today of all days, but he said instead, "So he's a fan?"

"Oh yeah. I even got him your jersey for Christmas. He's going to flip. He's with my mom right now, and I'll have Christmas with him when my shift's over at two."

"I have some posters, shirts, hats, and stickers over in my suit-case. Would you like to take him some?" He always tried to throw some of that stuff in his suitcase; that way, if he ran into fans, he could easily hand it out. He'd already left some with Gavin for his brother, Austin, and signed the logoed Bruins hockey stick Gavin had bought for his brother for Christmas.

Her face lit up then. "Are you serious? Oh my, he would go nuts."

Jag looked back at his family, who were watching him curiously. He took the cart full of breakfast and rolled it into the room a little bit. "This is my friend Tracy from high school," he said. "I'm going to go get her some paraphernalia for her son."

Her mom and Brielle both waved. "Nice to see you, Tracy," Brielle said.

"Merry Christmas," Mason added.

Tracy smiled and waved, stepping back from the door.

Jag headed across the hall to his suite.

"Did you ever get married?" Tracy asked.

Jag stopped next to his room door. He wanted to tell her about Faith and how he was going to marry her, but he just shook his head. "Not yet. You?"

"Yeah. A guy from Denver." Her smile disappeared. "Married and divorced a year later. I'd say it was the biggest mistake of my life, but I wouldn't have Josh without him." She leaned a bit closer and said, "Didn't you and Faith used to be close?"

He smiled. Maybe he could share that he and Faith were more than close now. She obviously hadn't seen Sheryl's article about them being engaged now.

"Did you know she married Blaine Grainger?"

The smile disappeared, and his gut tightened. "Yeah," he forced out.

"Man, that was so sad when he died. You should've seen them together. So in love they lit up the room. Couldn't take their eyes or their hands off each other." She winked as if they were sharing some joke.

Jag's stomach was full of lead now. He backed toward his door and opened it up with the key card.

"I've always thought if I could find a love like Faith and Blaine had, it would be the second miracle of my life." Tracy smiled more broadly. "The first was Josh."

Jag just held the door wide for Tracy. "Do you want to wait in here?"

She shook her head. "I shouldn't go in your room without another employee. I'll wait right here."

"Okay." He wondered if that was a company policy, but he thought it was smart to keep employees and guests alike safe.

He hurried through his room, trying to push the image of Blaine and Faith desperately in love from his mind. Faith had said that while Blaine had claimed to love her, she'd always been in love with Jag. But now Tracy was saying they'd been so in love that they couldn't keep their hands off each other? Jag didn't think he'd be able to eat any breakfast with those awful thoughts rolling around in his head. He wanted to storm to Faith's house right now and demand to know that she was telling the truth that she hadn't loved Blaine. If she was lying about that, could she be lying about how much she loved Jag? No. She couldn't fake the way she looked at him. Had she looked at Blaine the same way?

He took the stairs up to the bedroom two at a time. Shuffling through his suitcase, he grabbed one of each of the fan paraphernalia that he'd brought, and then he grabbed his wallet off the dresser, pulled out a couple hundred dollars, and hurried back down the stairs. Still reeling from Tracy's words, he pushed the door open and handed her all the stuff, shoving the bills in her palm.

"Wait, you don't need to ..." Her voice trailed off as her eyes brightened.

"I wanted to." He forced a smile. It wasn't her fault that she'd observed Blaine and Faith acting head over heels for each other. Maybe it was true, and Faith hadn't told him about it because she knew how it would hurt him. "Merry Christmas," he said to Tracy, raising a hand and walking back to his parents' suite.

"Merry Christmas," she repeated. "Thank you."

"You're welcome."

He knocked on the door, and his mom answered it quickly and ushered him inside. Breakfast was all spread out, and he mechanically followed his mom and started dishing up a plate. He sat down to eat, listening to his family chat and thankful they didn't seem to notice he was feeling off.

Mason was teasing his mom and Brielle. "Think how insane the presents will be on Christmas morning when your mom has grandbabies. We'd better get busy having some for her, Bri."

Brielle stuck her tongue out at him and turned on Jag. "I'm sure Jag is going to beat us at that."

Mason hugged her and murmured too loudly, "I think making grandbabies for your mom sounds like a great idea."

Brielle laughed and pushed at him. "If you sweet-talk ... maybe."

Mason pumped his eyebrows at the rest of them. "I'm great at sweet-talking."

"Stop," Jag protested. He liked to tease with them, but he couldn't dismiss the picture Tracy painted of Faith and Blaine. Watching Brielle and Mason light up the room was difficult.

"Mason started it," Brielle pointed out.

Mason shrugged and kissed her again. Jag concentrated back on the food. He was sure it was amazing, but it tasted like sawdust to him. Faith and Blaine couldn't keep their hands or their eyes off each other? His stomach churned.

His phone rang, and he hurried to pull it out. His agent. "Excuse me," he murmured to his family.

He went out into the hallway to have some privacy. If Mike was calling on Christmas morning, it must be important. Mike didn't have much family, but he respected his clients.

"Merry Christmas," Jag said.

"The story is breaking late tonight," Mike said. His voice was depressed and cautious, as if afraid Jag could jump through the line and throttle him. "They didn't want to do it on Christmas morning, so they're holding it."

"The story?" Jag crossed the hallway and entered his own suite; the hallway was still too much of a public place to chat with Mike. "Sheryl already shouted far and wide about me being engaged to Faith. I know she didn't spin it into great publicity, big surprise, but being engaged to Faith is solid, man. I know it'll help me look stable and a good bet to re-sign—"

"Not that story," Mike cut him off.

Jag waited, but there was silence over the line except for a few heavy breaths. "Mike ... what's going on?"

"Sheryl somehow got wind of the multiple sclerosis."

Jag heard a roaring in his ears and was hardly able to listen to the next bit.

"I got word from a contact at *The Rising Star* that the story is coming out. There's nothing we can do to stop it, but we can request a meeting with your coaches and the owner tonight, or worst case first thing tomorrow morning, and deal with the fall-out. Do you want me to call and charter you a plane? I'll set up the meeting. They all love you as a player, and I'm sure they'll come if they can. If we can tell them before the article comes out, it will be better, but I just ... don't know how it's going to go."

Jag could hardly comprehend what was happening. He'd worked hard to protect this secret. How? Who? He cleared his throat and muttered, "Yes, thank you, please charter a plane. Either out of Vail or Denver would be great." He paused, but he had to ask. "Did your contact have any idea how Sheryl found out?"

Mike let out another heavy sigh. "It's all in the article. Your fake fiancée was telling a friend, and Sheryl overheard. She makes your girl look like a gossipy gold digger."

"You're sure?" Jag could barely get the words past the tightness in his throat.

"Sorry, man."

Jag grunted something and hung up. He sank onto the couch and passed a hand over his face. Faith had told a friend? It wasn't nearly as bad as her telling Sheryl directly, but it still stung. He'd thought she knew how important it was to guard this secret. He'd entrusted her with it when he'd revealed it to his own mother. And she'd gone and blabbed about it to a friend? He wondered when. They'd been together almost nonstop since he'd revealed his secret.

He pushed his way to his feet and hurried up the stairs to the bedroom. He was going to shower quickly, tell his family good-bye, and then find Faith before he had to get to the airport. He understood rationally that she hadn't meant for this hailstorm to come down on him, hadn't meant to ruin his career, but he bristled at the idea that she'd casually chatted about his condition with someone and given Sheryl the golden ticket. It felt like almost as big of a betrayal as the day he'd heard she'd married Blaine.

Had she lied about her and Blaine's relationship like Tracy had alluded to? Had she lied about the letter Blaine left for her? He'd never actually read the letter. She'd pulled a letter out of her purse and then put it back in. What if it was all a farce, and the Dear John he'd gotten ten years ago had been from Faith? Could the woman he adored be manipulating him?

No! There had to be some other explanation. They loved each other. They were finally going to be together. Yet the horror of his awful thoughts and suspicions struck deep into his heart and gouged out any happiness he'd thought he would have with her.

As Jag finally made it out of the lodge half an hour later, he saw Gavin Strong on the steps.

"Merry Christmas." Gavin looked more animated than normal. "Thanks for the extra presents and signing that stick for Austin. You should've seen his face."

"I'm glad he liked it." Jag wanted to simply chat with an old friend, but he found he needed some confirmation. "You knew Blaine and Faith when they were together?"

Gavin faltered, leaning back. "Well, yeah. It's a small valley, Faith works for me, and they both went to our church."

"Did you think they were desperately in love?"

Gavin glanced away, obviously uneasy. He splayed his hands. "Hey, man, that's really not my business."

"But you did?" Jag pushed.

Gavin lifted his shoulders and met his gaze. The serious look in his dark eyes returned. "They seemed like a happy couple."

Jag's stomach pitched again. That was more information than Tracy gushing about how they couldn't keep their hands or eyes off each other. Gavin would never inflate anything. If they'd seemed happy to him, they must've seemed desperately in love to everyone else. Jag's jealousy reared anew, but especially because Faith had told him time and again how she'd never loved Blaine. Why would she lie about that? It made him doubt everything about their relationship now, and that was more sickening than the world knowing about his multiple sclerosis.

CHAPTER ELEVEN

F aith enjoyed the craziness of a Christmas morning with all of her rambunctious younger siblings. She'd spent the night at her parents' house, sleeping on mattresses pulled from all the beds that they shoved into the big living room in the basement. She stayed up late talking with her sister, Jaleen, about married life and all things Jag.

She could hardly wait to see him again, but it was good they'd given each of their families their time this morning. While she wanted to just be close to Jag at all times, she still wasn't sure how she could commit to flying to Boston with him tomorrow, leaving the spa and all her clients in a lurch, and maybe moving to Boston after they got married. His season could stretch until almost June. Could either of them stand to wait that long to get married? If they married during the season, she'd have to plan on sharing him with his team and his busy schedule, and she'd be alone in a big city while trying to find a job, friends, and her own spot with his regular church congregation. That all terrified her. Yet part of her was excited about the adventure of it all, especially being with Jag.

The doorbell rang as they were cleaning up breakfast. Faith's heart leapt. Was Jag already here? Three of her brothers fought their way across the room to open it. Brandon pushed Taft out of the way at the last minute, dodged in front of Isaac, and yanked it open. Her parents' main level was a large open area for the kitchen and living room, so she could see who was there from the kitchen sink.

The open door revealed the handsome face and perfect body she'd been hoping for. "Jag!" She started his direction, but her steps faltered as she saw the frown on his face. His blue eyes looked stormy and cloudy. "Jag?"

He glanced around at her family and forced a smile. "Merry Christmas," he said. "Can I steal Faith for a few minutes?"

A few minutes? She wanted him to steal her for life.

"Sure." Her mom gave him a big smile.

Faith walked on stiff legs toward the front door. She didn't even grab a coat, and she faltered again when Jag didn't hug her or even put his hand on her lower back. He held the door for her, waited while she walked through, then stepped out onto the shelter of the front porch. It was snowing, not hard, just beautiful, big white flakes. The house had been extra warm, so she wasn't immediately chilled by the cold, but she knew she would be soon.

"I should get my coat," she murmured, glancing up at Jag,

looking for some indication that everything was all right. What could've happened? Jaleen had told her there'd been some online articles about the two of them being engaged that hadn't been too flattering to Faith, but she didn't think that would bother Jag. Something was bothering him.

"Take mine," he grunted. He slid out of his coat and wrapped it around her shoulders.

Faith was embraced by the warmth of his too-large coat as she slid her sleeves in. "Thanks." It smelled delicious, like him.

He looked down at her as if trying to decide how to proceed. "I have to fly back to Boston now," he said.

"Right now?" She shivered despite the coat. "Why?"

He looked out across the snow-covered yard. "My agent got word that the story about my multiple sclerosis is going to be released tonight."

"Oh, Jag." She felt sick to her stomach. She tried to put her hand on his arm, but the coat sleeve was hanging past her hand, so she awkwardly rested the coat sleeve on his arm. She pulled it back and wished she could wrap her arms around him, but he looked too upset. Which was crazy. If he was so upset, why wouldn't he want her to hug him, comfort him? Something in his eyes and his demeanor told her to tread cautiously.

He focused in on her. "Sheryl somehow found out."

"Are you kidding me?" She couldn't believe it. "That woman is like the plague. How could she have found out?"

Jag kept looking around at the yard, as if something in the trees or the snow held the answers. Faith moved in closer, and his eyes darted to her, then away again. Finally, he muttered, "Apparently, she overheard you telling a friend."

Faith's stomach contracted and her heart slowed in its rhythm. She didn't care that Sheryl had accused her. She barely knew the woman, but she wouldn't put anything past her. She did care that Jag seemed to buy the lie. "And you believed that I would share your secret with anyone?"

Jag focused on her again. "I don't know what to believe. It's all messed up. How else would she find out? Only you, my family, my agent, and the doctors know."

"Maybe one of them told a friend, but I didn't." Her voice was as icy and as raw as the icicles hanging from the porch.

Jag jammed a hand through his hair and then folded his arms across his chest. "I know Sheryl has it in for me, but my agent checked. She overheard you, Faith."

Faith was so shocked she could barely comprehend what Jag was accusing her of. Flapping her jaw to some friend in a public place where that slimy reporter would overhear it and broadcast it to the world? She would never do that to Jag. "I already told you I didn't share anything with any friend. Why can't you believe me?" Faith was getting more upset by the second.

His jaw worked, but he didn't reply.

"You know what?" Anger and despair overtook her. Ten long years she'd longed for him, and now he'd let them blow apart because of a lying witch? She couldn't imagine how upset he was that his disease would be revealed to the public, but that didn't justify accusing her. "It doesn't matter, Jag. Go to Boston. Work things out with your coach. I'm really sorry that your secret is out, and I'm really sorry you'd believe Sheryl over me." She slid out of his coat, dropped it on the porch, and said, "I'm out." Turning, she wanted to just escape inside the house, go hide somewhere, and have a good cry.

"You were never planning to come with me to Boston, were you?" Jag's voice stopped her from behind.

Faith whirled on him. "You want me to come ... now?"

Jag shook his head shortly. "It hit me this morning what a sappy sucker I am. Anything you say, I believe, and I wait like a puppy dog for you to give a treat to."

"Excuse me?" She folded her arms across her chest, hugging herself for warmth and protection from his cold words.

Jag's brow furrowed. "I don't think you ever intended to come to Boston with me, to marry me. Was this all just fun for you? The superstar shows back up in town, and you think you'll get some good make-outs in, have your fun, and then wave to him as he leaves again."

"What are you talking about? I wouldn't just play you."

Jag moved in closer. He towered over her. "Like you didn't play me ten years ago? Like you didn't play Blaine? Did Blaine really rewrite our letters? Did he even leave a letter for you on his death day? Was your relationship really one-sided, or did you love Blaine as desperately as he loved you?"

Faith's heart was thumping so hard and fast she could hardly catch a breath. "How dare you?" she asked, panting for air. "You honestly think I lied about everything?"

He stepped back, confusion and uncertainty warring in his gaze. "I don't know. The Faith I knew and loved would never lie, but I don't know what's going on. It's all imploding." He threw his hands in the air. "Everything is falling apart around me. I can hardly think straight, and then people keep telling me how desperately in love you and Blaine were."

Faith stared at him. Who would've said that? She could see how that would make him doubt her word, as she'd told him they hadn't had a good relationship, but why wouldn't he believe her?

He hung his head, and his voice dropped and became almost gravelly. "I've loved you so long. I can't even comprehend that you wouldn't love me as deeply."

Faith's heart leapt at his last words, but if he couldn't trust her or trust how deeply she loved him, they had no kind of relationship. Her marriage to Blaine had been a farce. She couldn't handle a relationship with Jag if it wasn't built on trust.

Jag stared at her for several long seconds. His blue eyes full of sorrow and confusion. "I've got to go." He didn't promise he'd come back, or they'd try to work it out, or he was sorry for accusing her of lying. He simply swept his coat up and stalked away, his broad muscular back rigid and unforgiving. He climbed into the Audi sport utility, slid his glasses on, started the car, and drove away.

Faith sank onto her knees on the cold porch. She thought she'd found the love of her life again, but she'd been wrong. All she'd found was more heartbreak.

CHAPTER TWELVE

J ag was unsettled and nauseated as he shook hands with his coaches and the owner's representative, a lawyer, and sank into the plush conference chair. Today had been one of the worst of his life. He could only compare it to the day he'd gotten the letter from Faith writing him off and the day he'd heard Faith and Blaine were married.

He loved hockey and wanted to keep playing, but accusing Faith like he had, seeing the pain in her deep brown eyes, and then walking away was tearing him apart. If he couldn't play hockey, he'd survive. If he couldn't be with Faith, he was certain he'd become a shriveled, weak, angry man, even without the multiple sclerosis. Yet he was still hanging on to his anger, doubt, fear, frustration, and pride. What was it going to take to let it go?

"Mike informed us about the multiple sclerosis," Coach Hurley started without preamble.

Jag's gut clenched, but he kept his shoulders straight and nodded. "The doctors found it after the Islanders game."

The owner's representative, Mr. Truman, leaned forward. "Were you going to share the information before we signed a new contract?"

Mike gave him a warning glance, but Jag was way past hiding this. "No, sir, I wasn't."

Coach Gunnell's eyebrows shot up. "Why not, Jag?"

Jag looked at each of the three coaches in turn. These were men he respected, and he'd played his guts out for them. "I want to play hockey. I was afraid that if you knew the truth, you wouldn't re-sign me."

They all acknowledged this with either a nod, a shrug, or a compassionate look.

"Jag," Coach Weatherby said, "*we* want you to play hockey. I wish you would've come to us the minute you knew."

"Me too." Jag was miserable and humiliated; at the same time, he was glad it was out and he could just deal with it. He'd hated hiding this. "Honestly, Coach, I believe that I can still perform at top level for you. The issue with the Islanders game was only a bad case of the flu. That was when the doctor discovered the multiple sclerosis. Would there be any chance we could look at an altered contract?"

"Altered how?" Mr. Truman asked.

Jag looked to Mike. His agent didn't look thrilled, but he gave an encouraging nod. Jag went forward with some of the ideas he had. "Maybe take it year by year, or add a clause that if my specialist says it's time to be done, I'm done, and I repay the salary I didn't earn, or a clause that if the coaches are all in agreement that I'm not performing well, I'd be done. I'm happy to look at whatever options; I really just want to play." He'd made plenty of money, over fifteen million a year for the past five years, and he'd been able to pay off his condo in downtown Boston, a home in Boca Rotan, Florida, and invest an incredible amount of excess. It wasn't about the money.

The coaches were all looking at each other. Mr. Truman spoke first. "I think Mr. Jacobs would look at any of those options. He's instructed me to keep you if at all possible with your health."

Jag's breath came out in a whoosh. The lawyer didn't give off warm vibes, but Jag was tempted to hug him. "Thank you, sir." He looked to the coaches as well.

Coaches Gunnell and Weatherby were both nodding. "We'd be okay with that," Gunnell said, speaking for both of them. They swung to look at Hurley. "What do you think, Bob?"

Hurley appraised Jag. "You think you can still give me a hundred percent?"

"Yes, sir, I do."

His head coach stood and extended his hand. Jag stood as well, shaking it. Coach Hurley held on and looked him deeply in the eyes. "Next time, you come to us immediately."

"Yes, sir."

Coach Hurley released his hand and headed for the door. "I'm going back to my grandbabies. See you at practice tomorrow."

"Thanks, Coach."

Mike and Mr. Truman were talking quietly off to the side. They'd work out all the details, but Jag trusted Mike and was relieved with how this had all gone.

The other men shook Jag's hand, Coach Weatherby expressing his condolences that Jag had gotten the disease.

"It's a slow-progressing disease," Jag reassured him. "And I'm going to do everything in my power to stay strong."

"I know you will." Coach Weatherby thumped him on the shoulder.

Once the others had filed out, Jag turned to Mike.

Mike lifted his hands and shoulders. "Well, you just made more work for me with negotiating an interesting contract, and probably lost me some money ..." He grinned. "But you'll keep playing. That went as well as could be expected."

"I think so too."

Mike patted Jag's arm and headed for the door. "I'm getting back to my Christmas celebration too. Met a beautiful blonde a few weeks ago." He winked. "Did your family stay in Colorado?"

Jag nodded. "They'll be here on the twenty-seventh."

"Okay, get some rest."

Jag walked slowly out of the conference room, down the hall, and took the elevator down with Mike. They left the TD

Garden arena together. Jag was relieved and excited that he could continue to play, but he also felt very alone. That was crazy. His parents lived in Newport, Rhode Island, and Mason and Brielle lived in Atlanta, so he never had anyone living with him, but tonight he hated the thought of going back to his condo by himself.

If only Faith did love him as much as he loved her. He felt awful that he'd accused her of sharing his illness with a friend, but even more so that he'd said she'd lied about Blaine. Maybe she and Blaine had been ecstatically in love and she'd skewed that vision because she knew it would hurt Jag. He didn't want to picture them in love, but he didn't want Faith to be unhappy either—far from it. He wished her every happiness; he just selfishly wanted her to be happy with him.

It had killed him, though, when he'd said that he loved her and that it hurt that she didn't love him the same, and she hadn't even responded. He supposed she'd been right when she'd said a few days ago that there was too much garbage between them. He still loved her so much it hurt, but he didn't know how to act on that love.

CHAPTER THIRTEEN

Faith made it through Christmas only by hiding away from her family in the bathroom and breaking down a few times. She had the day after Christmas off from work, and she had no clue what to do with herself. Luckily, a couple of her younger siblings talked her into taking them snow-skiing at the resort. They had a great day together in the fresh powder, and she was grateful that it helped her burn another day without Jag. That night, she stayed at her parents again. She'd never loved being alone in the house she'd shared with Blaine, and she couldn't stand going there now.

On the twenty-seventh, she woke early. Stretching, she picked up her phone and noticed a text. As she clicked on it and realized it was from Jag, her heart walloped against her chest. It was a picture of him, obviously taken during a game, as someone shoved him into the wall. His gloved hands were both pressed against the glass, and his gaze was sad, longing for something.

Faith swallowed hard, staring at the picture for a long time. Did it mean what she hoped it meant? It brought to mind their old tradition of gloves on the glass, saying that nothing would come between them. Yet he hadn't sent her a loving note, asked her to come to him again, or told her he'd come to her.

Faith packed up her things and headed for work. She used the gym at the lodge to work out and shower and then went over to the spa. Her mind replayed the two times Jag had been here: once for his haircut and once when they'd used the pools together. She smiled wistfully. She was still angry that he could accuse her, but she couldn't stop herself from loving him.

Different clients came and went, and all she could think about was Jag and that picture. Shanna walked a nail appointment back at eleven that morning. Faith pasted on a smile to greet the client, but it froze on her face. "Brielle?" she whispered.

Brielle gave her a brief hug. "Hey, you."

"How's it going?"

"Horrible, actually, but I'm pretty sure you're going to help me make it better."

Faith's stomach lurched. She didn't want to ask her to clarify. Was Brielle going to try to get her to forgive Jag? Faith wanted to love him, but she also wanted to hold on to her righteous indignation. "What are you wanting to do with your nails?" she managed to ask.

"We both know I'm not here for nails, and I'm thinking you need to cancel the rest of your appointments today and tomorrow."

"I can't do that."

"Can't or won't?" Brielle raised a challenging eyebrow.

"Both. What do you want?"

"I want you to love my brother."

"I do," Faith flung at her.

"Enough to forgive him for being an idiot?"

Faith sank into the chair next to the nail station and shook her head. "It doesn't matter. He doesn't trust me. You can't build a relationship without trust."

"That's true, but we all make mistakes, Faith. Come with us to Boston and give him another chance."

Faith shook her head, biting at her lip to keep from crying. She desperately wanted to go to Jag, but nothing had changed. He'd only sent that one picture. He probably still thought she'd done all the awful things he'd accused her of.

"Faith." Brielle pulled a chair up, sat down close to her, and grabbed her hand. "I'm close to Jag. I love him so much." She gave Faith a piercing look. "He's loved you his entire life. It's finally your time to be together."

The words made Faith's heart leap, and combined with the picture he'd sent, Faith thought his sister was probably right. He did want to be together, but he didn't know how to navigate it any better than she did.

"Don't screw it up by being prideful and angry."

Faith's head bobbed. She didn't know what to say.

Brielle sighed. "I'm crazy about Mason—I feel so blessed to be with him—but he's still a guy. Let's face it: they do stupid crap sometimes, but because we love them, we let it go. That's how relationships are. It's never going to be perfect, but if you truly love Jag more than you love yourself, you're going to forgive him and make it work."

Faith was mulling over her words. She was holding on to pride and she could see she was being selfish, but she was still scared. "I love him completely," she admitted. "But what if I come with you and he doesn't want me?"

Brielle chuckled deep and low, then leaned forward and hugged her again. "Oh, Faith. That is the least of your concerns. The man adores you."

Faith blinked back tears. "If that's the least of my concerns, what's the biggest concern?"

"What are you going to wear to the game tonight?" Brielle winked.

Faith couldn't help but laugh. "I've got nothing fancy."

"We don't need fancy, but we do need you in some killer jeans, high heels, and Jag's jersey."

Jag's jersey. Faith wanted to wear it so badly.

"Don't worry. I've got you covered." Brielle stood and held out her hand. "Ready?"

Faith took her hand and stood, determination coursing through her. There was still a chance Jag wouldn't forgive her, but she had to take the risk. Life without him was no life at all.

J ag was warming up with the team. He felt great physically, ready to play after the break. Emotionally, he was still a mess. He no longer cared how Sheryl had gotten the information about his MS. She was a witch and got awful information about celebrities all the time. Jag only felt bad that he'd accused Faith. He'd wanted to just fly back to Colorado and beg Faith to forgive him, but there hadn't been time with practice yesterday and the game tonight. He couldn't get away until next weekend, and he didn't want the conversation to happen over the phone. He'd sent that picture of him, but she'd never responded. Maybe it was a stupid move, but when he'd seen that picture online a couple of years ago, it reminded him of the tradition he shared with Faith. Right now, he needed to know how Faith was feeling, hold her close, and beg her with his words, his gaze, and his body to forgive him. Maybe with all three, he'd stand a chance.

They were skating into a line for the national anthem. He glanced up at the box he had reserved for his family and friends. His eyes widened when he saw the long dark hair, the gorgeous face, and the perfect body ... wearing his number twenty-four jersey. Faith. Jag wanted to punch a fist in the air, throw off his gloves, and rush to her, but the national anthem was starting, so he couldn't do any of those things.

He took his helmet off, put his hand over his heart, and tried to focus on the flag and the words like he usually did, but his mind was racing. He hoped the founding fathers wouldn't find him disrespectful, but Faith was all he could think about. She'd come for him. It was the most amazing Christmas present he could think of. He'd known he loved her before, but it touched him deeply to see that she'd laid aside her pride and anger at his unjust words Christmas morning, flown across the nation, and now was here for him.

The song finished, and the announcer went through the Buffalo Sabres' starting lineup. Jag waited impatiently, and his gaze kept darting up to the box, where he was certain Faith was focused on him. He was always anxious before a game, but these nerves were out of control.

"And our favorite centerman, Jag Parros!" the announcer roared.

Jag skated forward, clutching his helmet in his left hand and his stick in the right. The crowd was screaming uncontrollably. He raised his stick, pointing it at his box. Faith leaned against the glass and pressed her hands against it. His heart leapt. Nothing could ever come between them.

"I love you," he mouthed.

Her answering smile was sweet, and he could see her mouth form the words too. She loved him. He'd waited so long, and he'd never been so happy. He listened to the crowd's cheers and just soaked it all up. He was going to keep playing hockey. More importantly, he was going to be with Faith. No matter what, he was going to make it work with her.

He jammed his helmet on and prepared to play. This game was going to be amazing, and the after-party with Faith would be even better.

F aith couldn't peel her eyes from Jag as the team warmed up and then stood for the anthem. She forced herself to look at the flag during the song, but then she was right back to staring at the man she loved. When they announced his name, he skated forward, raised his stick, and pointed it right at her. She put her hands against the glass like she used to do from a much lower position in high school, not this lofty box.

She saw him mouth the words, "I love you."

Faith's heart slammed against her chest, and warmth rushed through her. "I love you," she said back, aloud.

Jag grinned, shoved his helmet on, and prepared to play.

"Are you glad you came?" Brielle asked.

Faith smiled around at Jag's family. "Yes. Thank you so much for bringing me."

"Couldn't leave our future in-law behind." Mason winked.

Faith grinned, but then she turned back. She wanted to focus on the game. She didn't move from the glass throughout any of the periods, only taking breaks when the team did and chatting with Jag's family. Jag played brilliantly. The Bruins won 5–2.

As the game finished, she wondered how long she'd have to wait to see him. This huge stadium was set up nothing like the rink back in Vail where he'd played in high school. She couldn't just go down and wait by the plexiglass wall for him to slam into it.

She watched as the team skated through and slapped gloves with the other team. Jag was one of the last to go through. As he finished, he stared up at her, and his mouth formed the words like they used to: "Wait right there."

She nodded. She'd wait for hours if she needed to.

Jag's family chatted with her as she waited. She was anxious and just wanted Jag to be here. She loved his family, but she wasn't sure she wanted them to witness the next scene of her life.

Jag's mom pulled out her phone and smiled. "Faith, honey, we're going to greet Jag in the hallway and give you two some time alone. He wants to know if you'll wait here."

Faith's stomach leapt. "Of course. Thank you." She gave them all hugs, said her goodbyes, and then stood watching the open doorway. She could hear voices in the hallway; she was pretty sure Jag's voice was among them.

Shifting her weight from foot to foot, she clutched her hands together, and sweat beaded on her brow. She'd come for him, but their last conversation had been pretty horrible. Could they put that, and ten years of misunderstandings, behind them?

Jag's strong body appeared in the doorway, and every worry and misunderstanding disappeared. His dark hair curled slightly, still wet from the shower; his lips curved in a grin; and his blue eyes lit up. He strode toward her.

Faith smiled, fighting tears as how deeply she loved him washed over her.

Jag stopped right in front of her and held his hands up. Faith trembled as she placed her palms against his. He grinned, and then he wrapped his hands around her waist, picked her up off her feet, pushed her back into the glass, and proceeded to kiss her. Faith lost all ability to think, but she still had the ability to respond. And respond she did, wholeheartedly. His kiss lit up her world and told her that he loved her every bit as much as he claimed.

He pulled back and let her feet slide to the ground but kept her pinned to the glass. "Faith," he murmured. "You came."

She nodded.

"I'm so sorry. I was a complete idiot to doubt you. I was scared and angry and ..." He shook his head. "All I want is you, Faith. I can't tell you what it means that you came for me." His gaze swept over her and heated her clear through. "Wearing my jersey. I love you."

Faith wrapped her arms tight around his neck. "It's always been you for me, Jag. I want to be wherever you are, and I want to be with you."

His answering grin made her body tremble with anticipation.

"Will you marry me?" she asked.

Jag chuckled, low and deep. "Yes. Yes, I think I will."

There was no more time to talk, as he kissed her passionately. Faith held on tight and returned each kiss. She was finally with the man she'd been meant to be with. Brielle was right that it wouldn't be perfect, but Faith loved Jag more than she loved herself, and now she was exactly where she wanted to be.

EPILOGUE

Twenty-Eight Years Later

Faith held on to Jag's hand as a young man pushed the wheelchair, shuffling across the ice at the Boston Bruins stadium. She looked around at the cheering crowd. They'd had a lot of good memories in this arena throughout the years.

He grinned up at her. "Everybody's cheering for you, love. How does it feel?"

Faith laughed. "They're cheering for you, and you know it."

The announcer was rattling off all of Jag's accomplishments on the ice, as well as the contributions the Parros family had made to hockey throughout the years. Faith raised her left hand while Jag raised his right, waving to the crowd but still holding on to each other.

Jag had gone on to play five more years after they had married, and he'd retired when he wanted to, not when multiple sclerosis wanted him to. He'd fought hard throughout the years to stay healthy and fit, but the disease still progressed, and though he tried to only use a walker, the wheelchair was sometimes easier. They'd had their struggles throughout the years, but they'd done it together. Their son and two daughters were the icing on the cake. Faith's constant prayer now was that Jag had some more years in him. She hated the thought of him going to heaven without her.

The announcer roared, "And now your favorite centerman, Ryker Parros, will present his father with his retired jersey!"

The crowd was screaming so loud it was almost painful on her ears, but Faith ate up every minute of it. Her son skated confidently out on the ice. His massive frame, dark, curly hair, and bright blue eyes were all Jag; his full mouth and slightly upturned nose were from her. Her heart leapt as her boy skated straight to her, a huge grin on his handsome face. He'd played for the Bruins for two years now, and she and Jag couldn't be prouder.

Ryker reached her, bent down low, and gave her a hug. "Hi, Mama."

"Hi, sweet boy." She went on tiptoes. He was so big she was able to barely reach his cheek and kiss it.

He squeezed her tighter, and she loved every second of it. Hugging her tall, tough son was heaven to her.

Ryker released her and turned to his dad. Jag pushed to his feet and gave the fans a fist pump. They went nuts. Faith leaned close to hear Ryker say, "Hey, Dad."

Jag reached out his hand and grasped Ryker's shoulder. The two embraced. Faith could hardly hear Jag over the roar of the crowd. "I'm so proud of you, Ryker."

Ryker smiled, his blue eyes suspiciously bright. He handed Jag the jersey, and the crowd went even more wild. "Love you," Ryker said.

Tears were trickling down Faith's face as she watched the exchange. Ryker pushed back on his skates and waved to the crowd. Faith glanced up at their family's box. It was bursting at the seams with his parents, her mom—as her dad had passed away a few years ago—Brielle and Mason's family, some of her siblings and their families, and most importantly her and Jag's two beautiful daughters, Mylee and Avery. Her heart was so full of love that it might burst.

Ryker skated off to join his team before the next period started. She and Jag waved to the crowd as well. The young man who'd escorted them onto the ice rushed out to assist them. Jag sank back down in his chair. Within half a minute, the crowd's cheers had settled behind them as they were helped off the ice and loaded into an elevator that would take them back to their box.

Jag's eyes were shining as he tugged on her hand. "Come sit right here," he said.

The young man smiled and focused on the elevator panel as Faith sat on Jag's lap.

Jag grinned at her. "Much better." He might be weaker than either of them would have liked, but he was still strong enough to hold her close.

Faith kissed him softly and then leaned against him. "We're so blessed," she said.

"Yes, I am." Jag rested his head against her. "Yes, I am." He tilted her chin up and kissed her again.

Faith had no clue how long the young man waited to take them to their suite. She savored the kiss and the moment. Who knew how much longer she'd have Jag? She wasn't going to miss out on any opportunity to show him how much she loved him.

DON'T FALL FOR A FUGITIVE

"Do you have a novel, or seven, that you could leave with me to get through the day? I hate to be the one to break this to you, but the books on your Kindle app were ruddy lame, and I don't dare open my own phone for fear some technology will track me down faster than a police dog."

He smiled but pretended to be affronted. "My books are lame? You don't like *Marketing Rebellion* and *Mind Your Business?*"

"Blimey, no! I should care about reading those kinds of books. Maybe I'd find something that would help my own business grow, but I can't stand nonfiction."

"I guess we're going to have to agree to disagree yet again." He folded his arms across his chest and smirked at her. Hazel was struck again by how nicely muscled his body was, as he was wearing a fitted long-sleeved shirt and jogger-type pants. She admired his greatness too. Here he was teasing her when he could easily be turning her over to the police.

"Sorry," she said, "I can't do 'agree to disagree' about proper football or reading preferences. I'm one of those who believes everyone must agree with my theories." She winked to show she was teasing. In this diverse world, somebody would go insane trying to win everyone over to their way of thinking. "Don't worry, I'll lure you over to the dark side of a proper reading list soon."

"What's the dark side?" He leaned in closer, and she could smell his crisp scent again.

"Romance." She felt her cheeks heat up as his gaze took her in. "I mean romance novels, you know?"

"Hmm." He stepped closer, and she leaned against the bathroom counter with nowhere to go and no desire to be anywhere but here. "I could teach you a thing or two about romance ... novels, that is." His lips turned up in an appealing smirk.

"Could you now?" She held on to the countertop for support. It was either that or throw her arms around his neck and let him teach her exactly what he knew about romance. She guessed it might be a whole lot more than she knew. "Are you a big-time heartbreaker, Mr. Strong?"

He chuckled at that and eased in even closer. His chest brushed her arm and her breath hitched. "I'm not, actually, but I've read my share of romance novels."

"Liar," she threw back at him, grinning. "There was not a stitch of romance on that Kindle app. Pages and pages of business, marketing, and religious books. The most exciting thing I found on page fourteen was finally a Clive Cussler novel."

He chuckled. "You caught me."

"What am I going to catch you doing?" She was flirting as hard as she'd ever tried.

His eyebrows lifted.

The bedroom door swished open, and Heath wrapped his arms around her and swept her behind the half-open bathroom door so whoever had come in couldn't see them. Her breath whooshed out at the thrill of being so close to him. Her arms automatically wound around his lower back, and she pressed in even closer. Heath smiled down at her, and she could feel his heartbeat going almost as fast as hers.

Hazel attempted to calm her heavy breathing and listen to whoever might be coming in now. "Are there no locks on these ruddy doors?" she whispered.

Keep reading here.

HER CHRISTMAS WEDDING FAKE FIANCÉ

By Jennifer Youngblood

Hearing the ringing of the doorbell, Colin took brisk strides toward the door, the hard soles of his dress shoes clicking sharp tones against the wide-planked floor. Judy, the receptionist from the cleaning company, had called a few minutes ago, letting Colin know that the owner of Dust Busters would be stopping by. He could tell from the trepidation in Judy's voice that he'd upset her. Now that his anger had cooled, Colin felt guilty about going off on the older woman. Still, he was pleased to see that his phone call had gotten the attention of the owner. *The squeaky wheel gets the grease.*

He opened the door, steeling himself up for another confrontation. His jaw went slack as found himself staring into a set of bright green eyes, fringed with thick, dark lashes. His gaze flickered over the woman. Was she the owner? He hadn't given any thought to how the owner would look, but he hadn't expected her to be bombshell beautiful. At first glance, he'd thought her tall, but realized she was wearing heeled boots that gave her a good six inches. She was petite and curvy with long curly hair, tipped with blonde highlights. Her smooth, unblemished skin had a radiant glow. His gaze was drawn to her full cinnamon-colored lips. She thrust out her hand. "Hello, Mr. O'Brien. I'm Sofia Reed, the owner of Dust Busters." Her tone was brusque ... a little put out, maybe that she had to take time out of her day to deal with this matter. Well, it had taken time out of his day too. When you hired a cleaning company, especially one highly recommended, the assumption was that they would behave like professionals.

He reached for her hand, jolted by the spark that ran through him when their skin touched. Her delicate hand had a surprisingly strong grip.

Her eyebrow cocked in a question. It was then that he realized he was still holding her hand. He cleared his throat, releasing her hand. "Thanks for coming," he said as he stepped back and motioned for her enter.

"Of course," she said automatically, tightening her hold on her purse strap slung over her shoulder. Her voice had the husky edge of a faint Latino accent. He tried to pinpoint her ethnicity. She was part Hispanic. Her light eyes pointed to European heritage, as well.

She launched right into the conversation. "I understand you wish to speak to me about some difficulty that you had with your cleaning crew."

"Yes."

She eyed him in a challenge. "Would you mind telling me your version of the story?"

He rocked back, his jaw muscles pulling taut. "My version?" He didn't like the insinuation in her tone.

She lifted her chin. "Yes."

His brows darted together. "What did your workers tell you?"

"Before we get into that, I'd prefer to hear your take on what happened."

It was startling how quickly the scalding fury resurfaced. First, Beverly. Then, the maids. Now, this woman. Colin was starting to feel like all members of the opposite sex were out to get him. Straightening to his full height, he took abrupt, jerky steps into the kitchen with Sofia following behind him. He stopped beside the island and motioned at the open jam jar and the stacked slices of bread atop a napkin. "I got home from work early and came in here where I discovered them making lunch."

"That's your story, and you're sticking to it, huh?" A hard amusement shimmered in the depths of Sofia's eyes, washing them with a golden hue.

Colin flinched. "I beg your pardon."

She gave him a superior look. "No begging necessary."

The gall of this woman was astounding! His voice took on the sharp edge of a knife. "I don't know what you're playing at here, but I don't find it amusing."

She clutched her purse, looking him in the eye. "I was wondering the same thing. What're you playing at?"

The hair on the back of his neck rose. "I'm not the one with the defunct employees."

Her face turned red. "For kicks, let's say that the events happened exactly as you describe—"

"Of course, they happened as I described," he shot back. Colin didn't know if he should be impressed or appalled at Sofia Reed's insolence. "Are you accusing me of lying?" Colin couldn't remember the last time anyone dared speak to him in such a condescending way.

She held up her hands. "I'm not accusing you of anything. I'm only trying to get to the bottom of the situation."

Coming Soon!

ABOUT THE AUTHOR

Cami is a part-time author, part-time exercise consultant, part-time housekeeper, full-time wife, and overtime mother of four adorable boys. Sleep and relaxation are fond memories. She's never been happier.

Join Cami's VIP list to find out about special deals, giveaways and new releases and receive a free copy of *Rescued by Love: Park City Firefighter Romance* by clicking here.

cami@camichecketts.com
www.camichecketts.com

ALSO BY CAMI CHECKETTS

Strong Family Romance

Don't Date Your Brother's Best Friend

Her Loyal Protector

Don't Fall for a Fugitive

Her Hockey Superstar Fake Fiance

Steele Family Romance

Her Dream Date Boss

The Stranded Patriot

The Committed Warrior

Extreme Devotion

Quinn Family Romance

The Devoted Groom

The Conflicted Warrior

The Gentle Patriot

The Tough Warrior

Her Too-Perfect Boss

Her Forbidden Bodyguard

Georgia Patriots Romance

The Loyal Patriot

The Gentle Patriot

The Stranded Patriot

The Pursued Patriot

Jepson Brothers Romance

How to Design Love

How to Switch a Groom

How to Lose a Fiance

Billionaire Boss Romance

Her Dream Date Boss

Her Prince Charming Boss

Hawk Brothers Romance

The Determined Groom

The Stealth Warrior

Her Billionaire Boss Fake Fiance

Risking it All

Navy Seal Romance

The Protective Warrior

The Captivating Warrior

The Stealth Warrior

The Tough Warrior

Texas Titan Romance

The Fearless Groom

The Trustworthy Groom

The Beastly Groom

The Irresistible Groom

The Determined Groom

The Devoted Groom

Billionaire Beach Romance

Caribbean Rescue

Cozumel Escape

Cancun Getaway

Trusting the Billionaire

How to Kiss a Billionaire

Onboard for Love

Shadows in the Curtain

Billionaire Bride Pact Romance

The Resilient One

The Feisty One

The Independent One

The Protective One

The Faithful One

The Daring One

Park City Firefighter Romance

Rescued by Love

Reluctant Rescue

Stone Cold Sparks

Snowed-In for Christmas

Echo Ridge Romance

Christmas Makeover

Last of the Gentlemen

My Best Man's Wedding

Change of Plans

Counterfeit Date

Snow Valley

Full Court Devotion: Christmas in Snow Valley

A Touch of Love: Summer in Snow Valley

Running from the Cowboy: Spring in Snow Valley

Light in Your Eyes: Winter in Snow Valley

Romancing the Singer: Return to Snow Valley

Fighting for Love: Return to Snow Valley

Other Books by Cami

Seeking Mr. Debonair: Jane Austen Pact

Seeking Mr. Dependable: Jane Austen Pact

Saving Sycamore Bay

Oh, Come On, Be Faithful

Protect This

Blog This

Redeem This

The Broken Path

Dead Running

Dying to Run

Fourth of July

Love & Loss

Love & Lies

Cami's Collections

Steele Family Collection

Hawk Brothers Collection

Quinn Family Collection

Made in United States
North Haven, CT
09 November 2023